secrets & spice

A Playlist Kinda Love Story, Side B

d. allyson howlett

ISBN: 979-8-9852810-5-7 (d) 979-8-9852810-4-0 (p)

This work of fiction is created by D.Allyson Howlett and her 100% human imagination.

Cover Design: Sara Oliver Designs

Editor: Nicolette Beebe

Copy/Line Editor: Represent Publishing

Formatting: D. Allyson Howlett

*There is content in this book surrounding loss, trauma and self-destructive behavior that might be triggering to some readers. If you are someone who is struggling, I hope the resources listed below are your first step to living your best life.

https://recoverycentersofamerica.com/

https://www.samhsa.gov/

❀ Created with Vellum

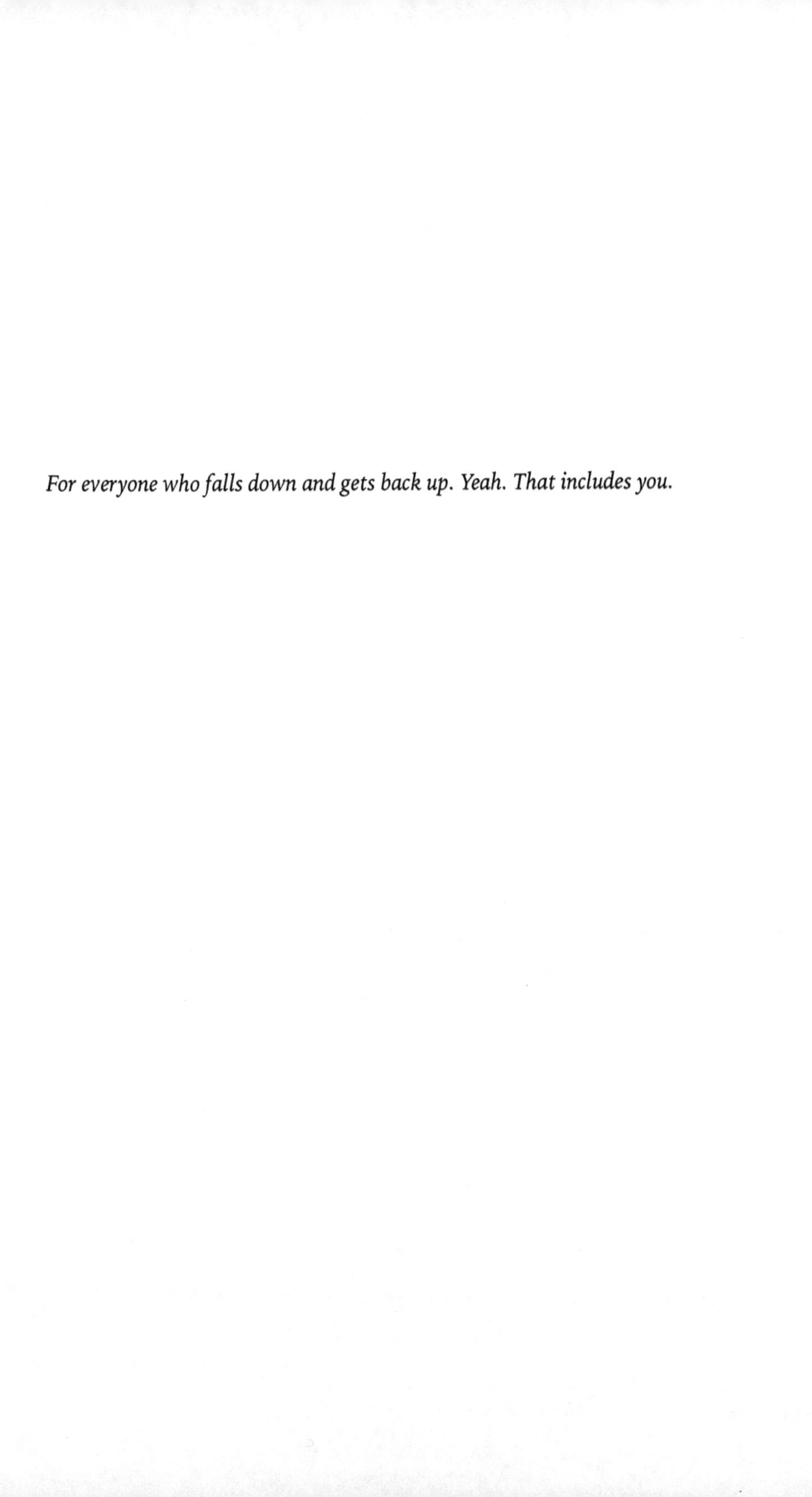

For everyone who falls down and gets back up. Yeah. That includes you.

And these children that you spit on as they try to change their worlds are immune to your consultations. They're quite aware of what they're going through.

— David Bowie

secrets & spice

one

. . .

new york, monday, july 6th

I COULDN'T WAIT to get out of here. Thousands of miles stretched between this town full of batshit memories and our refreshing destination of California. It took less than a month to get everything Pete and I needed together, including the money my dad had left me that would fund most of the trip. My dad had saved almost two years of college tuition for me after I turned eighteen. I wouldn't use it all, of course. And Pete chipped in some of his own savings. He didn't want to freeload like my slimy ex, Westley, would do. Just goes to show how different Pete and he are, and how messed up it was that I stayed with Wes for so long.

"Ashley!"

Rolling my eyes, I shut the car door of my newly traded used Subaru Outback and turned around.

My mom walked down from the porch steps. Her dark, frizzy hair was up in a bun, still wearing her scrubs from when she got home at 4:00 a.m.

"Yeah?" I asked.

"Did you call your brother? Go over the plan?"

I gave an autopilot nod. "I will, I will."

"Right now?"

"Yeah, alright. Stop heckling me so much." I glanced back at the small, two-person teardrop camper hitched to my car. *GoRVing.com* was a lifesaver. Relying on dirty motel rooms to crash for the night didn't compare to a home we could take with us. It was cheaper this way, and a hell of a lot more fun. Pete had never been camping before, so I'd have to show him how it was done. Not going to lie, it had been a long time since my last camping trip, but I wasn't worried. Thanks to Dad, I practically grew up outdoors.

I pulled out my newspaper-cased phone from my back pocket. With a quick swipe, I unlocked the screen and held down the side button. "Call D."

My phone flashed three blinking dots before it responded. "Calling D."

I enabled video chat and waited for Dimitri to show his ugly mug. The screen flashed to life, not focusing on anything remotely familiar.

"Hold on a sec." Dimitri adjusted the screen and finally settled on his giant head. "Okay, I'm good." He flashed a perfect white-toothed smirk. "What's up, Sis?"

He looked nothing like me, except for the shape of his eyes. His skin was darker than mine, matching that of strong umber, where mine was more sunset terra cotta. His hair was tight and curly, buzzed on either side and well-maintained. He had a firm jaw and a proud, wide nose. His cheeks rounded out his face, making him look too sweet to be a football player. Built like a tank, he put any linebacker he came across to shame.

"Geez, for a sweaty football player, you sure know how to keep your place tidy," I snickered.

"That's all Max." He sighed. "I'd be so bad if she wasn't around." He looked away for a second before returning to the screen.

I leaned against the car, watching my mom bring out another bag from the house. "I'm leaving as soon as Pete gets here."

"You two still plan on stayin' with us for a few months once you get here?"

"Yeah. We plan on arriving by the beginning of September. We have a lot of stops along the way. Ohio, Indiana, Wisconsin . . . the list goes on. If that still flies with you."

"You kidding me? Max is more excited than I am. We got the room. These off-campus apartments are a sweet deal."

"You treating that girl right, Dimitri?" Mom twisted her mouth.

"Relax, Ma. I ain't my dad."

Mom rolled her eyes at the mere mention of her first husband. "Thank god for that."

"Ash," Dimitri said, "call me every time you hit up a new state. You hear me?"

"I will. God, you sound like Mom."

Mom pressed her lips together, looking away with a hint of sadness in her brown eyes.

"I gotta go," Dimitri said. "Drive safely!" The screen froze and *Call Ended* flashed on the screen.

I shoved the phone in my pocket and turned to Mom, who still looked as if the dam would break behind her eyes at any moment. "Come on, don't cry." I stepped in and wrapped my arms around her, squeezing gently as hers came around me, too. I could feel a few wet tears fall onto my bare shoulder.

"I just . . . worry about you. After everything you've been through with Westley."

My teeth clenched at the thought of my last year of high school. It was definitely not an average year, but nothing in my life ever was.

"You don't have to worry about me." I know that was stupid to say. Most moms are worried about their kids.

"I'm just so glad you're not going alone." She pulled away to look at me with a smile. "And that Peter is such a nice young man."

There wasn't a single day since graduation that Pete had not been at my house. He wanted to make a good impression on my mom. She wasn't too keen on the idea of driving across the country with a boy, understandably. With all the Wes drama, she told me to stay away from boys all together.

"God, you sound like an old person."

"I am an old person!" She pushed me playfully, nudging a smile free. "You got yourself a keeper there. Your dad would have loved him."

I shrugged, squinting a bit at that notion. "You think?"

"Yeah, I do. He'd scare the hell out of him first." She moved a stray clump of kinky dark hair from my face, pushing it into my massive mane. "I can tell Pete really likes you."

"He doesn't hide it, that's for sure."

Squeezing my arm, I pulled my focus back to her. "Just make sure you're ready, hun. And be careful."

A pang of guilt twisted in my stomach. I knew what she meant, from a girl-meets-boy standpoint, but this connection I had with Pete felt like something deeper. Despite how much my mom and I didn't get along, she knew my impulses. I had a habit of painting this Bob Ross-esque masterpiece around the relationships and life I imagined for myself, only seeing the fluffy little clouds and happy trees on the horizon. I focused so much on the places beyond the foreground that I never saw the chaos brewing at my feet. Wes was the worst storm I ever tried to ignore.

It was different with Pete, but that fear still sat on my shoulders, pulling my head down to stare at the ground. It kept me from getting ahead. Be cautious, not careless. The trouble was, I was so used to being careless.

"I know, Mom." I nodded weakly. "I will."

I was running away to find my horizon, and I didn't plan on tying myself down to anything or anyone. It may hurt Pete for me to say it, but I needed to be upfront. Just two friends, cruising the open road with nothing stopping them. Though, I couldn't promise nothing intimate would happen. I mean, come on, a girl had needs.

He was such a nerd, in a heartthrob kind of way.

The crackling of pavement caught our attention as a black car pulled up behind the camper.

"Right on time." Mom kissed my forehead and waved as the car lurched to a stop.

The doors opened, and both Pete and his sister, Kim, jumped out from opposite sides of the car. His dad exited from the driver's side and came around to meet everyone on the sidewalk. He was the quintessential dad next door, light brown hair like Kim and lean like Pete. He had muscle tone, probably from all the walking he did as a mail carrier.

"Good morning, good morning!" he said rather joyously.

"Oh my god, Dad, you are so embarrassing." Kim rolled her eyes before reaching out to me to give me a hug. "You look amazing, as always."

Kim was the sister I wish I had. We would hang out sometimes, just the two of us. It was cool to have someone slightly older than me to pal around with who actually had their life together.

"Thanks. Love your jacket."

"Funny, cause it's yours." Kim tossed her mid-length hair to one side as she slipped out of the sleeves, handing it over. "A going away present."

"Shut up, no way." I admired the leather buckles and dark stitching along the edges. The zipper came up at an angle, allowing the corner to flap over if not fully zippered. I couldn't wait to put it on, so I tugged it over my purple halter top and admired myself in the window of the Subaru. It was nearing eighty degrees, but I didn't care. I was showing this off.

"Looks good on you."

Pete stepped out from behind her, his dirty blonde hair coming down just past the tips of his ears. Einstein, tongue and all, plastering his white t-shirt. His eyebrows raised, watching me ham it up in my reflection.

"You wish you could look this good." I smiled, turning to him with my head tilting over my shoulder.

His smirk ate away at me, black-rimmed glasses framing his eyes perfectly. He was just the right height that I didn't have to be on my tippy toes to kiss him, but just enough to brush under his nose. God, if our parents weren't here . . .

"Need an accessory?" He lifted Gremlin, our long, gangly gray and white kitten, up in his hands.

Without waiting for permission, I grabbed him and planted fifty kisses on his warm, fuzzy head. "I missed you, you little fuzz bomb!"

"He caught a few mice in the garage recently," Pete's dad added. "He's definitely been earning his keep at the Landon household."

"Better yours than mine," my mom shuttered. "When she brought that thing home, I wanted to grab my broom so fast!"

Pete and his dad started loading the car with his things while Gremlin settled in my arms, purring at max capacity.

"You take care of Pete while you're out there," Kim told me. "You know he's hopeless."

"Am not!" Pete came back around to where we were, holding out a little leopard print fabric shelf. "Look what I found at the pet store." His bare arms were tight around the box, showing off that baseball player physique I couldn't wait to have wrapped around me again.

"What the hell is that?" I asked as he opened the passenger side door of the hatchback. Leaning in, he stuck the shelf onto the inside window with what appeared to be suction cups. "That better come off."

"Relax, it does." Pete scooped Gremlin out of my arms and plopped his little body on top of the shelf.

Gremlin stood on wobbly legs, clearly uneasy about the ledge. But after a while, he settled down, sitting with his front legs tucked underneath his fluff.

"You think of everything, don't you?" I asked, narrowing my eyes.

"Honestly, I don't know what you'd do without me." There was that smirk again, the charming, eye-catching rise of his lips warming up his cheekbones. The careless me was ready to jump on him and kiss it right off his face, but I had to hold myself back. Not here in front of our parents.

The thought of telling him I didn't want to be "officially together" was making things so hard to deal with. He was such a nerd, with his glasses and a smart-ass t-shirt. Glancing in the car, I could see his skateboard propped on the floor in the back, his backpack teeming with colored comic books. I was sure I'd have the pleasure of hearing him narrate to me the entire trip.

What would someone like him want from a girl like me? A broken, overused tissue with both an out-of-control life and the hair to top it off. He came from a Hallmark card life, parents happily married and a sister who didn't run away across the country to avoid them. Good grades in school, baseball player. He was too perfect.

I just wanted to be alone with him to figure it all out. No distractions. Just us. As far away from anything remotely resembling home as we could get.

"Can we go now?" I pulled at his shirt, leading him to the passenger side door.

"I thought I was driving first?"

"No way." I shook my head. "I want this town to eat my dust."

"Get over here, first!" My mom snatched me up again, pinning my arms down at my sides as she wrung the life out of me. "Promise you'll at least text or I'll have the national guard after you!"

"Geez, yes!" I rasped, inhaling deeply when she let go.

"I'll miss you, short stack!" Kim gave Pete an indisputable hug before moving on to join my mom in her death grip. "Don't think I forgot about you!"

They both hugged me till I choked. Pete's dad shook Pete's hand, smiling as he planted his other hand on the side of his head. "Call your mom. She'll be worried sick about you if you don't."

"I will."

"As much as I don't want you to go, I'm proud of you, Pete. This trip is a big *what if*. But you're doing it. Something I was too afraid to do at your age."

Pete looked away, trying to hide the embarrassed look on his face. I could tell those words meant a lot to him. It was awesome he had such a great relationship with his dad, like I did.

"Thanks, Dad." Pete hugged him, not waiting for an invitation.

My mom surrendered me and walked to Pete, giving him a gentle hug. "I trust you. Be safe. Take care of yourself and her. And even that mangy cat."

"Ashley." Pete's dad wrapped his arm around the back of my shoulders for a squeeze goodbye. "Don't let him do anything stupid."

"I can't make any promises, Mr. Landon."

After securing Gremlin in his cat carrier, I climbed into the driver's seat, closing the door with a satisfying thud. Pete took the seat next to me, waving his hand out the window. We pulled away from the curb, leaving our families in the dust at the start of what could be the biggest adventure of our lives.

With a sigh, Pete's arm dropped as I pulled the car around the corner, making a break for the highway. "This is it."

"This is it!" I smiled, glancing at him. There was no putting out his light. He was as excited as I was.

"Only nine hours till we reach Ohio. Northern Midwest, here we come!" He pulled out his phone, shaking it in his hand. "I have a universal amount of totally awesome road trip music for our listening pleasure. What should we listen to first?"

"Let's wait a bit till we put anything on."

His brow furrowed. "Why would you want to wait? Driving in silence is the worst."

"Because . . . "

I turned down another street and pulled the car over, throwing the gear into park. Before Pete could even ask me what I was doing, I climbed over the divide between us and straddled him, forcing my mouth on his to grab a taste of his sweet lips.

His hands immediately laced around my waist, pulling me against him. Pete was clear we weren't ready to round all the bases yet. But every time, I could feel we were closer and closer to hitting home plate. I was hungry for it.

Screw being cautious. I could be careless . . . just for a little longer.

two

. . .

ohio, tuesday, july 7th

GREMLIN PURRED in the circled nook my arms had created as I leaned on my elbows, kicking my feet in the air. The camper was small, but I couldn't ask for a cozier setup.

The entire interior was a king-sized bed. Way more than we needed, but perfect since we had a little fur ball sharing our space. The walls curved upward, bending into a large window that was perfect for stargazing. Both a heater and an air conditioner sat comfortably on the wall, with a cabinet just above them. We used that for the cat box, which fit miraculously. Gremlin never had a problem accessing it either, making cleanup quick and easy. Two small shelves flanked the window and a little sill sat underneath with outlets. There was another window by the door, which was where Gremlin's cat ledge attached so he could lounge in the sun.

Outside, we had access to a small kitchenette with a sink, 2-burner stove, and a microwave. There was even a spot for a large cooler and food prep area, complete with a cabinet.

The stars were flickering between the faded tree line of our campsite. Pete was still outside, but the insanity of the day had knocked me out. We spent the whole day settling into our campsite, which loosely translated to me giving Pete a course in camping 101. Tomorrow, we'd make our first tourist stop at the Rock & Roll Hall of Fame.

Getting into my flannel shorts and cozy tank, I unlocked my phone and scrolled through my contacts to call Dimitri. Pressing the video call button, I waited for him to answer. His giant head finally came on, moving the phone around as he slunk out of the living room where his TV was blaring.

"Hold on," he said as he dashed into his small but spotless kitchen.

"What are you up to?" I smirked as Dimitri settled in a chair.

"Just chilling with Max. She's got some reality show on. Trust me, I'm glad you called." His eyes lit up when Gremlin's head came into view of my screen. "Aw, there's that little monster! Max already bought so much shit for that cat. I swear, she's never met him and she likes him more than me."

"Wow. Good to know how she'll be when she finally wants a kid."

Dimitri's dark eyes widened. "Don't talk like that, Ash. Don't give her any ideas."

"I wouldn't dream of it." Gremlin rubbed against my chin before settling in between my arms. "We just got to Ohio. Hitting up the Rock & Roll Hall of Fame tomorrow."

"You gettin' me somethin', right?"

"Probably."

His perfect white teeth spread across his face in sweet satisfaction. "Nice!" He shook his head with a breathless sigh. "Man, I wish I could go with you."

"I'll send you some photos while we're there."

A few silent seconds ticked by before he shifted his tone. "So, how are things with Pete, anyway? You two . . . like a couple, or what?"

I peered out the window where the fire still flickered. "No, just friends, I think."

"You think?"

I held my breath, trying to decide what to say next. Dimitri wasn't always there for me, but when he was, it was one hundred percent. Which is more than I could say for my other brother, Ty; that self-centered asshole. "I don't wanna commit to anything, you know? Not after all the bullshit with Wes."

"He knows that, right?"

Pressing my lips tight, I kept the bullshit from leaking out. I couldn't think about it, let alone say it. I could talk the talk but, sometimes, it was hard to push myself to walk the walk. The last two days had been perfect so far. Just doing our thing, nothing weighing us down. But it was a lie, an illusion. I knew I couldn't keep it up, but I wanted to. How shitty did that make me? Pretty damn shitty. A user. I'd used Pete way before our first kiss. Letting myself get carried away and not respecting his boundaries. Putting him in danger with Wes without caring if he got hurt. I knew I had him hooked, and I dragged him along, just like I was doing now.

Fucking bitch.

Dimitri shook his head. "Ash, don't be stupid. Look what happened with that prick, Wes."

"I know. I know. I'll . . . I'll tell him."

The gorgeous Maxine, with a Greek-goddess-like appearance, came into view. She had perfect olive oil skin with a Marilyn Monroe beauty mark naturally sitting on the right side of her nose. Her hair was long and curly, pulled to one side with large-framed glasses. "Ash! What's up?"

"Hey, Max."

"Enjoying the trip so far?"

"Yeah, it's going. Still got a ways to go."

"You're only young once." She pulled Dimitri's ear. "Don't keep this guy too long. I don't get him to myself too often. With all his football shit."

Dimitri glanced at her. "What about your cosmetology shit?"

"Yeah, what about it?" Her pink-glossed lips landed a peck on Dimitri's before she left the screen. "Talk to you later, Ash!"

With a small roll of his tongue, Dimitri raised a brow at me. "Sorry, Ash. Gotta split. Can't let that kiss go to waste."

I stuck my finger into my mouth. "Yuck, don't air out your dirty laundry in front of me. That's nasty!"

A chuckle escaped him as he leaned back in his chair. "You're right, you're right. Listen. I know you've been all over the place. Take it easy on this Pete kid, okay?"

"I'll try." I waved, lifting Gremlin up so he could flap his paw goodbye. "Don't do anything I wouldn't do!"

"No chance. Talk to you later, Sis."

The call ended. I swiped my phone back to the home screen. Pressing my finger on the gallery app, I scrolled through the photos of me and Pete from our journey so far. Being stupid in the car, pumping gas, showing off like an actual couple should. We looked so carefree, like nothing could have ruined the good times we were having. The thought tugged at my heart a bit.

I'd gotten too good at hiding things.

Sitting on my knees, I raised myself up to the long shelf along the top of the bed. My hand fell on a small wooden box I had slipped up there before we left New York. Looking down on it, I felt the smooth wood against my fingers, tracing the etching of my name across the front. My dad made me this box. With a harsh breath, I lifted the lid just enough for a little artificial light to filter through. The rush of blood picked up as the knitted outline of my woven bracelet came into view. That bracelet was worn to remember my dad. It was the last gift he'd ever given me, and after he died, it was the catalyst of my self-destruction.

How could something given out of love change me so drastically and become something I never wanted to be attached to ever again?

The day I took it off and placed it in this box was so freeing. But now, staring at it in the cold wooden coffin I'd banished it to, it had never been more tempting to put back on.

The door opened, and Pete dragged himself in. I shut the box and slid it back onto the shelf as he sat on the bed to take off his shoes, dropping them on the mat before closing the door. My blood pressure slowed at the smell of campfire smoke overtaking the cabin. It brought back memories of roasting marshmallows and listening to my dad tell scary stories by the fire.

"I need to brush up on my fire making skills."

I leaned my head in my hand and turned toward him. "You telling me you weren't a pyromaniac when you were younger?"

"Uh, no. I'm not nuts." He took off his jacket, shaking any ash free from his messy blond hair.

"Loving fire doesn't make you nuts."

"I'm assuming you've had experience with this topic?" Pete eyed me suspiciously as Gremlin bounded to him, rubbing his furry love all over Pete's extended hand.

A sly smirk graced my face. "I may have lit my living room rug on fire when I was a kid."

"I knew you were insane." Rolling across the bed, he came to rest right beside me.

I looked away from him, remembering my brother's words. *Take it easy on him*, yeah right. We would be stuck together for the entirety on this road trip. Why stir the pot and make things awkward?

"Hey." Looking up from my internal monologue, Pete held out his hand. Two white earbuds sat in his palm. "Wanna listen?"

Taking one, I popped it in my ear with a smirk. Pete took out his phone and scrolled through the plethora of music he had stored up for the trip. "Any requests?"

I shook my head. "You know what I like."

He glanced out the stargazer window, raising his eyebrows, along with his smirk. "Well, I hope this is a good choice, then." He put the earbud in and laid down under the window.

I came in close, nuzzling against his shoulder as the music churned into our ears. Laying against him, I draped my arm across his chest. The powerful scent of smoke escaped from his hair. Drawing into his warmth, the cool waves of M83 made the stars dance like crystal light. Pete's arm came around me, bringing me right against him. Gremlin attempted to squeeze between us, falling over and coming to rest against my back.

I should tell him right now. Before I waited too long and convinced myself not to. *Why couldn't this be enough?*

Maybe if I so fucked up, it would have been. But as much as severing my ties with Wes was a defining moment in the life I was leading, it wasn't the final one. Forgetting, was it even possible? Moving on seemed like an eternity of struggle and more added bullshit.

The problem was, I didn't want to move on. I wanted to stay in this bubble forever, with Pete's arms around me, staring at the stars. But that was a far cry from reality. Because tomorrow, I would have to get up and live again. Another day waiting for the inevitable to happen. And I didn't even know what that inevitable was going to be.

I had to figure it out and hope like hell that I didn't screw up.

three

. . .

ohio, wednesday, july 8th

IT WAS A LITTLE NUTS, standing in the shadows of youth-filled oppression. Looking up, I admired the visual interpretation of Pink Floyd's "The Wall". The song pulsed into my ears thanks to my red Beats headphones. Chords matched the words graffitied on the white of each carefully constructed block that formed the artistic wall of society's expectations. A creepy sculpture guy in a suit hung down to glare menacingly at those passing below him. The glass ceiling of the Rock & Roll Hall of Fame, where the wall was housed, was a nice added touch, letting the Ohio sun stream down and catch on the wall's polished surface.

Pete came around from the other side, his phone in hand, probably snapping a million pictures of this thing. It was epic. This was a place I wished I could have been, had I been alive in 1990. A performance by one of the best bands that ever graced the planet, squaring their jaws and belting out melodies right in front of the Berlin Wall in Germany before it was torn down.

"Did you get a look at the teacher troll?" Pete came next to me, scrolling through the images he had captured on his phone.

I pretended not to hear him, though it was hard to ignore his innocent nerdiness. He was beaming. That cheeky smile of his made me wish no one else was around so I could kiss it off his face without risk of public indecency.

"I can't believe we're actually here. The Rock & Roll Hall of Fame."

I had to release myself from my daydream about Pete with that comment. It was pretty fantastic. "Visiting the Rock & Roll Hall of Fame has been on my bucket list since I was 9 years old."

"Seriously?"

I nodded. "My dad was a music producer. He always wanted to take the family here."

"Whoa, what?" Pete put his phone in his jeans pocket. "How come you never told me this before?"

"It's not like I enjoy talking about my dad. Brings up too much shit." When his lips tightened, I nudged him with my shoulder. "Lighten up, Pete. I'm not gonna start bawling my eyes out or anything."

When I said it, it sounded okay, but as soon as he put emphasis on the fact that I was talking about my dad, it changed. He wasn't prodding. I had brought it up, not him.

The subject of my dad was precious to me, like a really expensive gem I kept hidden under the floorboards. It exposed my soft side. The side I would rather keep hidden. There were barriers I broke with Pete that hadn't been for so long. Even though months had passed since we'd known each other, the need to justify my integrity and grit would never go away. Not even with him.

He adjusted the strap of his backpack, eyebrows raised. "You sure?"

"What? You're serious?" I placed my headphones back on my ears and rounded the wall to the other side, toward the stairs leading to the next floor of rock and roll legends.

I knew he wasn't trying to annoy me, but I didn't need his sympathy. Pete was a guy who actually listened and gave a damn about me, something I wasn't exactly used to. It brought the ungrateful bitch out, dragging my fear to the forefront of my mind. I'd never be good enough for a guy like him. There wasn't a shred of me that deserved Pete.

"Come on, Ash. I didn't mean it like that." Pete's hand grabbed my arm. Not like an asshole looking to swing, but with a gentleness that made the hair stand up on the back of my neck.

I looked around at him as he dropped my arm carefully. "I know, I just. Sometimes I don't know how to handle you."

He smiled. "That makes two of us."

I dragged my headphones off my ears and sighed. I still hadn't told him what my expectations were on this trip, and it was eating away at me. Dragging this out was a bad idea. I let my desire and stupidity get in the way. Willing to ride, but never willing to pay.

"Listen, Pete—"

"Say no more." He took my hand and gestured his head up the winding stairs of the building. "I think I see Bowie on the ramp." He pulled me toward it. "Let's just have a good time, okay?"

Tucking a strand of hair back behind my ear, I widened my eyes as I let my head fall to my shoulder. "Let the good times roll."

We made our way to the open staircase to ascend to the floor above. "I wonder if The Cars are in here? They should be if they aren't."

"We'll add it to the suggestion box before we leave."

"They have those here?"

"They sure as hell better."

I tightened my grip on his hand as we walked up the stairs. Being beside him, Pete's warm smile pushed away the urge to run from the gutter of my thoughts.

"Hey."

Pete's voice pulled me back from my zone out session. I could tell he was trying to read me. How I wish I could be alone right now, but being in the middle of Cleveland with cars zooming by as we waited at the crosswalk, there wasn't much opportunity to be alone.

"You okay?"

With a weak shrug, I glanced at him before looking back at the flashing red hand to ward off jaywalkers. Traffic was pretty heavy, and the sky was growing grayer by the second. I could smell rain in the air mixed with car exhaust, cigarette smoke, and the occasional whiff of roasting cart food.

"Here."

Before I could look at him, Pete shoved something in my hands. Instinctively, I grabbed it, looking down at the black plastic bag in my hand. "What is it?"

"Just a little something I thought you'd like."

Great. With a heavy sigh, I shook my head. "You don't have to get me anything, Pete."

"I know, but I wanted to."

I handed it back to him. "That's . . . nice, but I can't take it."

A chime rang and the red hand changed to the white walking man to let the foot traffic migrate between sides. Not waiting for Pete to take the bag, I shoved it back into his hands and made my way across. My arms were tight at my sides, and I swear I didn't blink. This was too hard. I waited too long to tell Pete that I didn't want to commit. Now he thought we were something without even saying we were.

Stepping up on the curb, I kept my pace until a hand grabbed the crux of my arm, pulling me into a small outdoor seating area in front of a restaurant.

"Okay, now I know something's up." Pete let me go and watched for my reaction, his eyebrows raised and arms folded.

"I just don't want any shit from you, okay?"

"So, I can't buy you things? Why am I barred from gift giving? Does it give you a rash or something?"

I tucked some strands of hair behind my ear, looking up into the water-filled clouds while I bit my bottom lip. I couldn't wait this out any longer, but he might decide to leave. Ditch me for being such a shit bag. I knew I'd ditch myself.

I came back down from my selfish ledge, knowing that I had to face him and suck it up. His mess was mine, after all. "I don't want us to be . . . us."

Pete glanced to the side, one brow raising. "Meaning . . . "

"I don't want to be together, okay? I need to detach myself from someone for a while."

"Oh." The confusion instantly melted into disappointment, his eyes dropping about an inch down his sullen face. There was nothing I could do but watch him, his mouth tightening as his gaze darted across the concrete.

A few drops of rain touched on my cheeks and bobbed at the ends of my hair. Shifting underneath one of the large table umbrellas, I released a long, drawn-out breath. "I'm shit. I know."

Pete looked back at me. "Why didn't you tell me this *before* I got in a car with you to travel across the country?"

"Because I knew you'd split."

"You knew, or you *thought*?"

I hesitated, realizing I was doing it again, assuming without really knowing. This is exactly the behavior that made the whole Wes thing so messy. I had to stop falling into this endless cycle of acting before thinking. "All right, I thought. But it's true. You wouldn't have come with me if I told you."

He shook his head. "Can't you give me a little credit? I would have understood if you told me instead of stringing me along like . . . " He huffed, shifting in his stance as he puckered his lips. "So, you just wanted to use me, then?"

"No! I mean . . . I like you, Pete. I do."

"Like, huh?" A harsh groan rumbled from his throat as he took the gum out of his mouth. The rain was coming down harder now. He moved underneath the umbrella, shoving his chewed gum back in the wrapper and pocketing it. "Could you knock me down any lower?"

"I know, and that's why it was so fucking hard to say anything to you!" Running my hands across my forehead, I took a deep breath to calm the rush of adrenaline surging through me.

I didn't deserve him. Shit, I didn't deserve anyone to be nice to me and get me gifts.

"All that bullshit with Wes. I just need to know what it feels like to be free for a while. If you don't want to stick around, that's fine. I get it. But I can't say yes to what you want right now."

The rain picked up, splattering on the surface of the umbrella that shielded us from above. Staring into his deep brown eyes, I waited on the edge of my hypothetical seat as my heartbeat radiated in my ears and tried to burst from my chest. I didn't want him to go, but I didn't want to lie to him either. Lies always hurt someone. I lived off of lies for the last two years of my life. It was hard getting used to the truth. Truth was an angel and lies were the Devil. In my head, the Devil always won.

The tightness in Pete's shoulders fell, his eyes blinking away the frustration he carried for my immature ways. "I won't leave you by yourself. That's not what a friend does."

The air caught in my throat. "You're serious?"

He pulled me closer to the table as the downpour set in. "Yeah. I'm serious." We both smiled at each other. "So, this free thing, that means no gifting or other recreational activities? I need to know the rules if I'm going to abide by them."

A light chuckle escaped my lips. "Just have fun. No strings attached. No commitment needed."

"No strings, huh?" He brought the gift bag into view. "That means you can accept this, then."

"Hmph, I guess I can."

Reaching over, I took it from him, opening it to find a classic prism Pink Floyd sweatshirt.

"Figured you could use it on those extra cold western nights."

"Shit, Pete." I looked back at him. "You know your stuff."

He shrugged. "What can I say? I'm just a swell guy."

"Swell? You really are a full-blood nerd."

"The fullest." He took a step toward me, his fingers falling onto my wrist. "I can still kiss you, right? No strings attached style?"

He tugged at my arm, which brought me closer as I fell against his chest. Looking up, there wasn't anything I wanted but to let myself get lost in his taste again. "You sure you're okay with this?"

He waited for a moment in the rain, holding me with his arm around my waist. "I get it. And yeah, I'm okay with it. I mean, I'm going to change your mind. You know that, right?"

My lips rolled between my teeth. He might not have to try. Fuck it, I might change my mind right now. Some girls would say I was crazy for letting a guy like him just sit on the sidelines, and maybe I was. Crazy to leave the door open, knowing that one day, he might step through it and I'd never see him again. But I had to do this for myself. Drop the old and put on a new face, a new Ashley that actually could stand on her own without the secrets and the rumors dropping with every step. I may be tough and stubborn as hell on the outside, but inside, I was still that 14-year-old kid who lost her dad, crying under her blankets alone in her room. I needed to stop relying on other people and start relying on myself. No one could save me but me.

"You can try," I whispered as I shortened the gap between us.

"Friends with benefits. I feel like we're in a sappy Ashton Kutcher movie."

"Shut up, Pete." I closed my eyes, letting the watermelon taste of his gum-soaked lips eat away at me. The perfect taste of summer.

four

. . .

illinois, monday, july 14th

THE ILLINOIS SUN WAS BRUTAL, beating down like a little kid burning ants with a magnifying glass. Throwing my hair up in a bun didn't help in the slightest. Fanning myself with the map of the Cahokia Mounds, I tried to keep pace with Pete as he scurried along the wide open space of this national landmark.

The air was dry and desolate over the rolling hills of countless remains of physical structures that once stood there. And by remains, I mean giant mounds of earth with nothing on them but french fry grass that crunched under my Converse. It was hard to picture the grandeur of what this place once was back in its heyday, before the Europeans came over and shut every Native American civilization down.

We didn't bother to stop in Indiana on our way here, so it was a straight six hour drive after our last few days in Ohio. It proved to be a flat drive as the landscape rolled by the windows of the Subaru. Once I stepped into the sun, it might as well have killed me on the spot. It didn't seem to deter Pete at all. Though, thank god our campsite had electricity hook-ups. I would welcome running the AC after trekking around this massive landmark for the next few hours. We cranked it on for Gremlin's sake before we left. Didn't want that little guy to suffer the same fate as us.

Looking over this mostly barren landscape, I adjusted my aviator sunglasses and peeled the strap on my halter off my skin. Even with shorts on, it was brutal. We were heading toward mound forty-seven or maybe thirty-eight? I stopped counting after the fifth one. Or maybe it was the first? Clearly, walking through over twenty acres of massive hills in the blistering sun was not my idea of a good time. But Pete was adamant about exploring some historical landmarks on this trip. I couldn't disappoint his nerdy little heart and say no.

"Can you slow down? It's not like we'll miss anything worth seeing."

Pete glanced back at me. "This place is historical, like America's version of Machu Picchu."

I rolled my eyes. "I think you're exaggerating just a little there, Pete."

"Look." He pulled me over, opening the map for my sun-shaded eyes to glance over. "This place was bigger than London at one point. A huge bustling city that thrived for almost a thousand years."

Pulling down my shades to make sure he saw my enthusiasm, I took a step back and swept my arm through the air. "And all that's left of it are these giant mounds of dirt?"

Scrunching his nose, Pete shook his head. "Do you enjoy taking the grandeur out of life's experiences?"

"I would be impressed if there were standing remains or something like that," I said, crossing my arms. "Do you see anything impressive like that around here?"

"That's what imagination is for. You read books, right? Without pictures, I assume?"

"Look who's talking, mister comic book."

"All right. Bad example."

Leaning forward, I let my hands fall on his map, folding it

haphazardly back into his hands. "Well, while you play boy scout, I'm gonna go find some shade."

"Stick around, will you?" He quickly opened the map. "I think Woodhenge is coming up soon."

"Woodhenge? Is that like Stonehenge, only with wood?"

"Well, yeah. Wooden poles. That . . . aren't there anymore."

I smirked, raising my hand into the air as I turned toward a line of trees sitting just at the foot of another mound. "Have fun with that!"

With a bounce in my step, I hurried to the minimal solace the trees would provide. Pete didn't follow me, likely thinking it was better not to be around me while he was searching for pole holes in the heat. The dried grass crunched beneath my Converse. Bending down, I ripped some free, rubbing them between my fingers. Sharp and brittle, like straw, they fell into pieces from my palm. This land was begging for rain, pleading for it.

Drawing near to the extended branches of shaded paradise, my phone buzzed in my back pocket. With a sigh, I pulled it out, seeing Amber's shining face flash on the screen. Swiping right, I popped on the video chat, being sure to keep the sun well behind me.

"Shit, it's bright there." Amber had cut her hair. It was short and becoming, accentuating the roundness of her face. She was walking somewhere outside, seeing the sidewalk pass behind her and the phone bouncing with every stride. She had on a lightweight jean jacket, which would be suicide in this place.

"You don't know the half of it." I finally settled under the tree, which offered only a small shred of relief. Beads of sweat trickled down the back of my neck, following the divots along my spine and into the fabric of my halter. "It must be 103 degrees out here. Or at least it feels like it."

"Where are you again?"

"Illinois. Some Native American spot Pete couldn't wait to see."

"Sounds boring."

"Yeah, I guess it is. It's giant man-made hills and walls of dirt." I turned to survey one of those very hills, smack dab next to the trees I'd adopted as my saviors. It was bigger than the other ones we've seen so far, making it a bit more impressive. As much as I didn't want to venture into the blistering sun again, I had the urge to scale this native mountain. "Here, let me climb one of these and give you the lay of the land."

Amber smirked. "I'm shaking in my boots with excitement."

As I stepped back into the sun, I immediately regretted my decision. I wanted to get this over with as quickly as possible. The hill was mostly flat. Aside from the dead grass that covered the mound, there were no potholes or slight curvatures to be felt.

"You're drinking water, right?"

"Shit." I looked down at my denim messenger bag. "Pete's carrying my water."

"And where is he?"

"Looking at holes in the ground. Literally."

"How are you two, anyway? Still holding on to the friends with benefits thing?"

"He respects my decision and seems okay with it."

"Is that true, or are you just telling yourself that?" Amber stepped off a curb into a crosswalk.

"I don't know half the time. Typical me, right?" I reached the summit of the hill. There was a slight breeze, which cooled the drying sweat on my skin. The refreshing air filled my lungs and a deep sigh escaped my lips. "It's actually really nice up here."

"Turn the camera, let me see."

Tapping the button to flip the view on the screen, I held the phone out over the landscape beyond the hill. Despite the sun's brutality, it stretched out toward the horizon like a sea of wheat. The mounds in sight rolled across the plain like waves in the water. And the breeze carried the harsh scent of scorched sand the beach could only match. "It's like a golden ocean." If it weren't for the breeze tickling my senses, I would have forgotten to breathe.

Like watching a movie and an epic shot of the landscape sweeps across the screen. Endless and impossible all at the same time. "I see why Pete wanted to come here now."

"Snap a pic."

"With you on screen?" I turned on the phone and flipped the camera into view.

"Yeah, it will be like I'm with you there. A girl can pretend, right?"

Shaking my head, I stepped down along the hill. "Let me find a sweet spot." After a few more careful steps, my feet fell on a landing just before touching down on the other side. Flipping the screen, I held it up, pointing at the camera with the horizon behind me. "Say cheese."

With a quick click of the finger, I snapped a shot that hopefully didn't make me look like a drowned rat. Turning the phone back around, I adjusted the camera again. "Acceptable?"

Amber stepped into what looked like a clothing store, the door shutting behind her. "Someone totally photo bombed you."

"What?" Navigating to the gallery, the picture came up with my smiling face. Sure enough, there was a guy peeking around the side with two fingers up and a smirk on his face. "Little fucker."

I turned around to overlook the landscape and there were three guys milling about in the grass, close to the shabby-looking path to the right of the mound. "I gotta go, Ash. Catch you later."

"Later."

I ended the call and finished the descent down. Sliding my phone back into my pocket, I walked straight toward the culprit and his posse with my arms folded. One of them glanced at me, saying something to the others.

He had short, sandy brown hair brushed to one side, his Adam's apple prominent against tan skin. The solid blue t-shirt he wore showed off the slight build in his arms and chest. As I drew closer, he took off his slick sunglasses, flashing his dark oval-shaped eyes. A sudden pinch twisted my stomach. If it weren't for his squared jaw and average height, he'd look just like Westley.

Holding my breath shook that annoying pinch free as I planted my heels. "Hey." All three looked at me, but the Wes look-alike smirked. "You think you're funny or something?"

"Why? You think something's funny?"

My eyes narrowed as I tried not to let his sarcasm ruffle my feathers. "Your face, maybe."

The other two chuckled, leaning back on their feet to control their reaction. One with light brown hair down to his shoulders and a Texans hat on sucked in some air and heartily smacked the culprit's shoulder. "She's all you, man."

The two walked on down the path, leaving the photobomber left to stand on his own two feet. Fishing for my phone, I pulled up the photo and shot it in his line of sight. "That you?"

He nodded, combing his hair back with his fingers. "You caught me."

"Any reason for poking your face into my business?"

"Whoa, pump the brakes." He held up his hands as I pocketed my phone again. "It's just a harmless photo bomb."

I think his resemblance to Wes was getting to me. My finger was constantly on the trigger, ready for any situation. That and this unbearable heat was not helping. I had to let up a bit. "I could have needed that picture for something important."

"What are you, a journalist or something?"

"No." I crossed my arms. "But I could be."

He watched, the corners of his eyes narrowing with his obnoxiously growing smile. Clearly, he was getting off on this. Maybe pushing his way into the line of sight of strangers was some sort of sick pleasure for him. He was just some snarky punk. And I was not in the mood.

"Look, I apologize. I didn't mean to show up in your important business."

I pressed my lips together and tightened my arms around my chest. "Now you're just being a smart-ass."

"Smart-ass. Funny face." His hands came up and down at his sides like a weighted scale. "Which one is it?"

His brow raised, cooling off the sweat building along my hairline. I don't know if it was a faulty memory or what, but it twitched the corner of my mouth, sending my hand to my hips. He was cute, I'd give him that. Charming even. Kind of like Pete. Or even Wes, before he got mean. I tilted my head above my right shoulder, slightly popping my hip to my left. "It could be both. It's possible."

An airy breath escaped him. "I'm sure you've handled plenty of the kind."

"Maybe." I shrugged.

"Hey." Pete's voice turned my head as he jogged up next to me, holding out my purple water bottle. "You might need this." I took it from him, bringing the spout to my lips and taking a relieving chug of insulated hydration.

Pete glanced at the stranger in front of us. "Hi."

The culprit's posture changed from somewhat relaxed to a little on edge. "Hey." He looked from Pete to me as I brought the water bottle away from my mouth.

"And you are?" Pete looked at me, his forehead slightly wrinkled with curiosity.

I raised my sunglasses and popped them on my head. "Some dude who photobombed me while I was video chatting with Amber." I smirked and watched the Wes look-a-like comb back his hair yet again in his uneasiness.

"Yeah, sorry about that." He extended his hand to no one in particular. "I'm Axel, by the way."

Pete took it like any nice person would. "Pete." He dropped his hand and looked at me. "And you've met the tiger."

I pushed against Pete's arm. "Tiger? Please. I'm more like a harpy."

"Surprised she didn't gouge your eyes out." Pete glanced back at Axel.

"I guess I didn't work her up enough." Axel looked at me. "Sorry, again." He backed up toward the path. "I gotta catch up to my friends."

"All right. Have a good one." Pete waved.

With a slight gesture, Axel shoved his hands in his jersey shorts pockets and continued on. I watched for a moment before turning to Pete's still-smiling face. "Having fun, are we?"

"You know me." I grinned.

"You could be nicer to complete strangers."

Pulling at his shirt, I led him back out toward the rest of the hills. It was kind of fun messing with Axel. He enjoyed the attention until Pete came around. Clearly, he thought I was alone and possibly available. But I would never go for a guy like him, evan though he caught my attention. "Trust me, I could have been much worse."

five

. . .

illinois, monday, july 14th

I SWEAR, these campground showers were a miracle. Walking back to the campsite, I ruffled the towel through my clean, damp hair. It was still grossly hot out, as far as evenings go. Though a gentle breeze cut away the dryness, which tickled the still moist skin of my arms.

It wasn't too dark yet. The sun painted the sky red and purple as it sank into the treeless horizon. The campground itself was flat. RVs upon RVs with tiny little spaces between sites gave it that suburban Long Island feel. It wasn't the most ideal place to stay, but it had facilities we needed after weeks on the road. Showers and public restrooms and a laundry hut. Our little camper sat on the outskirts, along one of the few stretches of grass the grounds offered.

The roads were half gravel, half paved. Despite its concrete appearance, it was incredibly litter-free. That and the street it was off of had a convenience store and a motel just a stone's throw away. This was one of the few places we'd be staying along our route that was so urban. Way more remote locations were in our immediate future, so I would enjoy the hell out of it before we moved on.

My flip-flops slapped against my heels as I made for our little site.

Pete sat in a foldout chair with a comic book in hand, held up against the armrest. He looked up at me with an immediate smile. "Don't you look refreshed."

"I never knew how amazing a public shower could be." I pulled up another chair and sat across from him. Draping the towel over the back, I put my toiletries basket under the seat. Wearing my gray shorts and Hicksville Comets t-shirt, I took a deep breath and closed my eyes. "I bet it's not this hot in New York."

"It's dry heat. I never thought I'd miss Long Island humidity."

I watched him as he went back to reading. Loose-fitted sweatpants and a dark t-shirt left him content in his chair. His dirty blond hair uncombed but clean. I could smell the Oars + Alps body wash he used from where I sat. "Tell me a secret."

Pete glanced at me with that cute little smirk on his face. "A secret, huh?"

"Yeah, a secret. Something you wouldn't tell anyone. Ever."

Gingerly, he closed his comic book and slipped it behind him. "I'll tell one if you tell one."

"Fair enough." Leaning forward, I rested my elbows on my knees, cradling my face in my hands. "You first."

"Fine." His eyes wandered a bit, teeth pressed into his lips, making him a tad irresistible. It took some time for him to land on something, but he finally came back from his wandering mind. "I did shrooms once."

A snicker escaped me. "Shrooms, like . . . magic mushrooms?"

"Yeah," he said in an exhale, almost comically. "Wasn't my idea."

"Let me guess." I raised an eyebrow. "Logan?"

He nodded, not even trying to save his best friend's reputation. "That obvious, huh?"

"Well, well, well." My arms folded as I leaned back in my chair. "This ought to be good. Imagine clean-cut Pete tripping out on psychedelics. Do continue."

He raised his glasses a bit. "10th grade. He got them from his older brother. Logan didn't want to do them alone, so I said I would try them, too. Stupidly."

"What happened?"

He hesitated, playing with the strings of his pants. "I can't really remember. I woke up on the roof of some random house. No shirt on with cereal and milk all over me. Logan was in a bush . . . way worse off than I was."

Laughter rolled me in my chair, pinching my gut so hard I thought I'd fall out of it. "Oh, man! I'd pay to see you flying on those."

"You've ever done it?"

Wiping tears from my eyes, I allowed myself to breathe. "No. But I've heard stories. Shit, Pete. You're braver than I thought."

As my vision came back from my watering eyes, I could see Pete sitting all rigid with his eyes focused. He was trying to look serious, but his chin quivered, forcing an exacerbated sigh muffled with laughter from his lungs. "I wouldn't recommend it. I think that is the only thing Logan will ever take to his grave."

"I bet you never touched them again after that."

"I touched *nothing* after that. Period." His fingers raised off his lap. "I swore off illegal substances after that fruitful experience."

Pulling my legs up, I leaned on my knees and shook my head at him. "Don't worry. I won't tell anyone."

He watched me, his baby browns full of kindness. Even though he seemed a little embarrassed to admit what he had done, he didn't shy away from telling me. That was not something anyone would be proud to admit, any sane person, anyway. The willingness to let me in on his secret meant something.

"Now it's your turn." He turned his chair fully around to face me, adjusting himself on the armrests.

Lifting my chin from my knees, I bit the inside of my cheek. I didn't intend to share anything personal with him, but now I felt compelled to do so. Not that shrooms were that dark of a secret. But it was for him. I didn't need him to tell me it was. I couldn't match that with something as simple as I hate the Harry Potter series or I could write with my toes. As much as I tried to wrack my brain for material, only one thing surfaced. A lie that I told him when I still felt ashamed to be near him. "You know when I told you I didn't screw around with other guys?"

"You mean, when you ambushed me at Grasshoppers?" he asked.

"I didn't ambush you." I sank back in my chair, remembering the first time I walked into his place of employment. "I was curious."

"Would you have gone to a comic book store if I wasn't there?"

I hesitated. By this point, he might know full well why I went to the comic book store that day. Because he got between me and Wes that night on the street. And I wanted to know what kind of person would do something so stupid and so incredibly selfless. Especially for someone like me.

"You know why I went in there, right?"

Pete gave a single nod. "You wanted to see if I was real. Like an actual person who gave a shit. Maybe clear the air about what Wes had said about you. I didn't understand why you cared, though. You didn't know me."

My stomach tied in unmanageable knots. What would he think of me after this? He already knew I didn't fall into the category of outstanding citizen, but this degraded me on a level I never wanted to remember I was part of.

"Maybe I wanted to know you." I swallowed hard, closing my eyes as I prepared myself for what I was about to say. "Wes said you were my fuck buddy. And, even though you clearly weren't, I told you I didn't do shit like that." Fear crept into my words as I dared to look at him. "But I lied. I wasn't screwing around then. But I have. In the past. After my dad died."

His arms settled into his lap.

My legs slid to the ground. "I was messed up after he died. I didn't care about myself. Screw the consequences, you know? I did so much stupid shit and gave things away that I should never have given away. To guys who didn't even know my name."

"How'd it end?" he spoke calmly.

My lips rolled between my teeth, nails digging into my legs. "Westley. He ended it. Dimitri tried, but I was too stubborn to listen to him. Wes was the only thing that worked." I looked down, feeling my legs shake. "As much of an asshole as he turned out to be, he saved me. In a lot of ways."

It was quiet for a minute, maybe five. I couldn't sense what Pete was thinking, or if he even cared. That was dumb. Of course he cared.

"Well, I'm glad he did."

My head shot up. "You're glad?"

"Yeah. Even though it didn't turn out well."

My hands balled at my thighs. A hot spark fired up my insides, sending my heart thundering against my chest. The chair fell over as I stood with haste. "That doesn't bother you? That I was a slut for most of my teenage life?"

He shrugged, straightening his posture. "Why would it bother me?"

"Because I'm no good for you! I don't fucking deserve anything from you!"

His face was calm and patient, which made me want to punch him so hard. "Is this another attempt to push me away? When you've already forced me to take a backseat? Why does it matter if you deserve me or not?"

"Fuck off, Pete!" I came at him with my finger raised. "Fuck you and your goody-goody attitude. Your perfect life with your perfect family and your perfect friends!"

He shot up off his chair and took my wrist.

"Get your hands off of me!" My hand connected with his chest as I tried to pry his fingers off.

"Stop!" His hands came around my shoulders, squeezing me together as I tried to force us apart. "You're not the only person in the world who ever screwed up."

"I *am* a screw up. Everything I do, everyone I know eventually sees it. And they run away or treat me like the bag of shit that I am."

"That's not true. And you know it."

Standing on my tiptoes, I clenched my eyes shut. "Yes, it is!" I kept myself there for a moment, feeling the pressure of his hands on my shoulders, forcing my breathing to slow down. That unrelenting fear crept back through me. It had not ended with Wes like I hoped it would. It was worse because there was no excuse now. The only thing left of that past was me. And I didn't want it. Not a single part of it. But it would never leave. It would always be there.

"Look at me." Pete's voice hit my face like a warm glow. "Ash. Please."

My eyes cracked open as I came back down to earth. His eyes kept my focus.

"Stop letting the past define you. It's not who you are anymore. Let go of this idea you have, that you deserve nothing. That's bullshit. Always will be." His warm hands cupped my face. "You deserve to be happy. Whether or not that's with me."

A quiver overtook my words. "I don't want to hurt you."

"Then don't."

"It's . . . unavoidable."

He gathered me up in his brawny arms, holding me so close I thought I'd fall right into his body and become part of him. "A Breakfast Club quote, huh? You're totally pulling a Claire right now."

I couldn't help but let a soft chuckle escape. Dragging my wet face across his chest, I let my weakness hold on to the strength I no longer had. Why he offered it to me is something I'd never understand.

Healing, after being wounded for so long, sucked. Sometimes it was easier to stay broken, but other times, it was nice when someone held you together.

six

. . .

illinois, thursday, july 16th

JUST DRIVING. The windows were down with my feet kicked up on the dash. I sucked on a cherry Tootsie Pop as the wind cut through my hair. My sunglasses deterred the glint of the midday sun, making it possible to take in the sights. We were on our way to Minnesota, making a two-day stop in Madison, Wisconsin. Maybe four days. It wasn't like we were on a tight schedule.

Riding along I-90 was a farmers paradise. I'd never seen so much open land in my life. It stretched on forever. Every so often, a tractor or silo would come into view. The midday sun warmed the fields as they rolled on and on, one into the other. Some were just cultivated earth, but others thrived. Truly endless.

My phone rang, so I rolled the window up to reduce the background noise. I clicked accept. "Hey, D."

"Yo, Ash. What's going on? Where you at now?"

"Heading to Wisconsin. We're on the road." I glanced at Pete, who seemed very content in his current driving state.

"Put me on video. I wanna see where you are."

I turned the phone around and pressed the camera button, flipping it so he could glimpse at the open road. "Holy shit! There is nothing there!"

"I know, right?" I smiled as I pulled the phone across the window toward the windshield. "It's crazy."

"Yo, Pete!" Dimitri held his hand to his mouth, like the volume button couldn't control his loudness. "I see you."

I turned the phone, so it was pointing at Pete. He grinned, raising an eyebrow as he glanced at the screen. "What's up?"

"Ash driving you crazy yet?"

"Crazy is a constant for her. It doesn't stop."

Dimitri's hearty laugh erupted from the phone. I twisted my mouth, glaring at Pete as his smile only widened.

"She's lucky she's cute," Pete said.

"Hey, that's my sister you're talking about."

"Shut up, Tri," Max's voice chimed in. "Hey, Pete. How's the trip so far?"

"Pretty interesting. As it should be."

I turned the phone back to me. "Why do I feel I'm gonna regret staying with you guys when we get there?"

"What? Nah, Sis. It'll be fun." Dimitri tilted his head, a trait I got from him. "Pete and I are gonna bond over football. I can tell."

"Football? No way, my sport is baseball through and through." Pete spoke loudly so they could hear.

"It won't be long till you're watchin' the games with me. You'll see." He laughed again as Max pushed against him gingerly.

"Drive safe, you two." Max giggled innocently. "And call us when you get to your next destination."

"All right, catch you later."

Dimitri focused the phone back on him. "And do everything I would do. Or maybe you shouldn't." He raised his hand. "Keep an eye on her, Pete!"

"Sure. Bye, guys."

I disconnected the call, letting the phone fall into my lap. Cracking the window again, the rush of wind whipped any loose strands of hair across my face.

"I think I'll get along with your brother," Pete said with a grin. "And Max is like . . . supermodel pretty."

"I know, right?" I leaned back in the seat. "It's a sin to look as good as she does."

The car grew silent. I gazed out the window, watching the land roll on like a constant stream. I was feeling better since the other day. The breakdown came out of nowhere and I realized just how much I was still trying to avoid. My past happened. You were what you came from. I believed that, maybe a little too much. Tons of people came from shittier situations than I had and could move past it. I was carving my own way.

The *why* was clear, but the *how* was something I was trying to figure out.

"Hey." I rolled my head off the headrest. "Sorry about being a total bitch the other night."

Pete glanced at me. "Don't apologize for how you feel."

"I know, but . . . I didn't mean to come down on you like that. I shouldn't have."

He shrugged. "It had to come out eventually, everything you've been keeping in. I'm glad it was me."

I squinted. "Why?"

"Because," he looked at me again, "I can catch you when you fall."

Shit, the things he said got my heart working overtime. He was too good to be true ninety-nine percent of the time.

"Stop being so fucking nice all the time, Pete!" I slapped his shoulder, making him flinch with a nervous smile.

"I'm driving here!"

"Tell me I'm shitty once in a while. Please!"

"Fine, you're shitty! You're the shittiest shitbag in all of shit town."

"Thank you!" I unbuckled my seat belt and pulled myself across the median between us, grabbing his arm. "Now tell me something I don't know."

The car swerved a bit as I kissed the back of his ear, dragging my teeth across the lobe and rolling it between my teeth. It was insane how quickly I went from zero to a thousand with him. He was like a drug I couldn't quit. It might have been bad for me, but goddamn it, the feeling was unmatched.

"Whoa, whoa." The car came up along the side of the road, bumping across the rocks and sand before lurching to a stop. I barely waited for him to switch the gear to park before climbing onto his lap, drawing my lips to his. His hands slid under my shirt, holding onto me with such desire it only deepened the kiss. Pressing against him, I took his face in my hands and held him there as his hands traveled up my back. Pulling away was the worst thing in the world, but a girl's got to breathe.

"This is . . . very dangerous behavior," he whispered. "But I like it."

"Yeah?"

"Do it more often."

"You'd like that, huh?" We kissed again. This time I didn't hold back, and neither did he. I wanted to live inside his kiss. The watermelon taste of summer intoxicated me into another realm of longing I had yet to experience with him.

He fished under my arms, prying me off of him. "Wait. Wait. Wait."

"What? What's wrong?"

"Nothing. I just." He took a deep breath. "You're gonna make me lose my shit."

"And that's a bad thing?"

"No. God no. But I don't wanna push it. Not yet."

Looking up, I couldn't really wrap my head around what he meant. "You still wanna wait?"

"Yeah." Pete gave a weak smile. "I mean . . . I don't want this to be the first time we take that step. Not here."

I settled down in a slump. No one's ever asked me to wait before. My gaze moved to the window, the flat land and rolling hills now frozen in the moment. "Is this because of what I said? About me being . . . promiscuous?"

"A little." I moved to get off him, but he grasped my waist. "But only because I don't want you to regret it. I would never take advantage of you."

I rolled my head back and forth, exhaling the last strain of sex-infused adrenaline from my body. "Okay. I get it." I bopped a finger on his nose with a smirk. "That's sweet of you."

"Well, I'm sweet on you, so." He sighed. "Trust me, I want to."

I wasn't used to this kind of treatment. Being respected and putting me first. This just goes to show how different Pete was from all the other schmucks I played around with. It was alien to me.

"So," Pete sat up from under me, "wanna hit the road?"

I looked over my shoulder at the empty road ahead. It sloped down about 30 feet from where we parked. "Not until you ride that hill."

"What?"

I whipped around as I grabbed his shirt. "Ride the hill. On your skateboard."

Lifting the handle on the car, I jumped out the door, walking into the street as he followed me out. The wind cut through us as we ogled the yellow lines of the highway.

Pete's eyes widened as we approached the drop, seeing how steep it would be for a car, let alone a guy on a skateboard. "That looks very unsafe."

"You can do it. When are you ever gonna get another chance?"

He looked at me, the nerves present in his laboring breath. I took his hand, raising a suggestive brow. The corners of his mouth pulled upward as he yanked me into another long and lasting kiss before letting go and walking back to the car.

"Put a helmet on!" I laughed as he frantically grabbed his gear.

"Trust me. I am." He slapped on his helmet, clipping it shut, taking in all the air the wilderness offered in the wind.

"All right. Let's go!"

Throwing the wheels on the pavement, he rocketed forward, dragging his foot across the highway to gain speed. I ran behind him, lost in the grand stupidity of this. Once he hit the tilt, he leaned into the grind, propelling himself forward at incredible speed. I stopped at the edge, watching him bow and glide like the pro he was.

Exhilaration echoed through the openness before us and I jumped in the air, raising my hands in victory. "Woo!"

He made it to the bottom in stride, letting the momentum take him. But he must have lost his balance because his foot came off the board, forcing him to mock run before stumbling completely and falling to the ground, skidding across the surface on his side.

"Shit."

I ran to the car and turned on the engine, flooring it forward down to where he lay.

When I came up beside him, I put it in park and bolted from my seat, leaving the door open as I bent down to his heaving form.

"Are you okay?"

He said nothing, eyes still closed.

"Pete!"

As quick as a snake strike, he grabbed me and pulled me on top of him, uncontrollably laughing as he practically crushed my lungs. "That was fucking amazing!" We both sat up together, his right arm still around me as our laughter settled. "You're amazing."

I let out a breathless sigh, bringing myself in, curling around him as we shared another perfect kiss.

If I could choose a day to relive a hundred times over, it would be this one. No chains, no surprises. Nothing but me getting a taste of a love I never thought I deserved.

seven

. . .

minnesota, wednesday, july 22nd

THIS PLACE WAS BUSTLING in every direction. We have officially crossed the Mall of America off the bucket list. Three floors of shops, food stops, and restaurants. Not to mention the aquarium on the bottom floor and the amusement park on the main. *An amusement park*. Rollercoasters, merry-go-rounds, zip lining, bumper cars, and anything else you could think of. Even the smell of cotton candy and fried food filled the area, smack dab in the middle of the entire mall. Rows upon rows of steel scaffolding protected a massive glass ceiling. The largest coaster wrapped around the entire length of the amusement park, sometimes weaving in and out of other rides, like a rush of wind through the trees.

We were waiting in line at the *Krusty Krab*, because apparently, Nickelodeon had a heavy hand in designing this place. There aren't many people who could say they actually ate a Krabby Patty. Wanderlust definitely paid off, even if this was the only thing accomplished during our entire trip. I'd call that a win.

"They even have kelp chips," Pete said while pointing to the overhead menu.

I smirked, leaning into his shoulder. "I bet you're gonna order one of everything."

"Nah. I'm saving room for some bubble tea from that place we passed."

"You're the only person in the world who would drink bubble tea."

"If I was, there wouldn't be a bubble tea place here." He looked at my slight amusement at his immaturity. "What? They heard I was coming and assembled one in anticipation of my arrival?"

I slipped my hand in his sweat jacket, running my fingers around his back. Getting right against him, I tipped my chin to rest against his chest, looking up at his sly expression. "You're such a nerd."

"I already know this." His arm came around my waist, fingers gracing the skin under my tank top.

That watermelon scent escaped with every exhale. It made my hair stand up and my heart skip. Nothing could keep me from pressing my lips against his. Not that he objected. Once our tongues folded together, that sweet summer taste kicked up the volume. Coming up on my tiptoes, I leaned into him, deepening our little play date. His hand squeezed me against him as my fingers dug into his back.

Situations like this were dangerous because when I fell into the trap, I forgot how to pull myself back out. It was a place I enjoyed being, wanted to be, every moment of the day. A place that left my damaged way of thinking by the wayside. Any shift from it, my brain would work overtime again, laying on the guilt and pleading with me to break the walls down instead of building them back up.

Pete's hands softened around my waist, pulling away to catch a breath. "Slow down, Ash. As much as I don't want to stop doing that, we aren't exactly alone."

"What? You're not up for educating these people on the definition of PDA?"

"More like the definition of how babies are made."

I crept in for more, but Pete only granted me a soft peck, keeping me at bay. "I promise, you can do that all you want once we're back at the camper."

Twisting my mouth into a scowl, I came down off my tiptoes and crossed my arms. "You're no fun."

The line moved up, and we went along with it. Looking out into the mall, the rounded ticket kiosk sat smack dab at the main entrance. A few people stood around it, waiting to purchase their tickets or wristbands, depending on how much you wanted to spend. There were three guys waiting there, talking in a group amongst themselves. One of them looked vaguely familiar. It wasn't until he turned around that I could see his face. Light brown hair and oval-shaped eyes gave away the Wes look-alike all too well.

"Shit." I pointed toward him to show Pete my discovery. "It's that guy from the Cahokia place."

"Weird. A little creepy, too." The guy at the counter called out for the next person to order, which was us. Pete slowly made his way forward. "Go say hi. I'll order the stuff."

"Why would I want to do that?"

"Don't, then." He stood at the counter. "Two Krabby Patties, an order of kelp chips. Actually, make it three patties—"

I glanced from Pete to Axel, my curiosity getting the better of me. "I'll go over there, I guess. See if he's stalking us."

"Sounds good. I'll catch up."

I pressed on toward the kiosk. My hair bounced at my shoulders, now long enough to dust the tops of them. I slowed down once I got closer, my purple converse gliding across the floor with a screech. The noise caught their attention. All three of them looked over.

Axel's brows raised in surprise, a nervous smirk flashing at the corner of his mouth. "Hey, it's the harpy."

"What are you doing here?" I crossed my arms. "You following me or something?"

He glanced at his friends. "Why the hell would I do that?"

I shrugged, kicking at the floor before crossing my ankles. "I don't know. You tell me."

The kid with the Texans hat cracked a grin. "How do we know you aren't following us?"

"I don't even know you."

"I'm Nate." Nate pointed to the third party-goer. "This is Curtis. And you already know Axel."

Curtis flipped his long, dark hair away from his wide face. He had some crude facial hair going on. It made him look grungy, but not in a bad way. And he was tall, taller than Pete even. "Sup?"

"I never got your name, actually." Axel drew my attention to him, eyes keenly focused.

Tilting my head, I glared at him. "You don't need to know my name."

"So, this is a one-sided conversation, then?" Axel glanced back at the other two.

"We're gonna hit up the coaster." Nate adjusted his hat atop his shaggy brown mop. "You wanna join us?"

I shook my head. "I'm not the kind of girl who allows herself to ride with strangers."

"Funny."

"You never answered my question." I focused back on Axel, who still looked like he was having too much fun. He was so distracting I couldn't handle it. "What are you doing here?"

Shoving his hands in his jeans, he mirrored my head tilt. "We're on a road trip, if you must know. We just toured the East Coast and are on our way back home."

My eyes widened as I straightened up. "Where are you from?"

"California." Axel squinted. "And . . . you?"

Both Curtis and Nate backed away. "Catch up with us later, all right? Bye stalker." They waved half-heartedly and left us standing in front of each other.

I hesitated, picking at my cuticles. There was no reason to tell this guy too much, but it was cool to meet someone on a similar journey. Taking to the road, not being tied down to anything. "New York. Heading to California."

"Road trip with your boyfriend?"

An instinctual 'yes' sprang to mind, but I shook it off like a dog riddled with fleas. Twisting my locks between my fingers, I leaned to the left as I mustered collective control over the situation. "Yes, to the road trip part. But no, he's not my boyfriend."

Axel stared at me, his eyes flashing. "Oh. You guys seemed like you were . . ."

"We're what?" I folded my arms, bringing the tough girl out to keep me together. The old part of me felt a small attraction toward this guy. The part that fell in love with Westley after he swooped down and rescued me from a fiery pit of destruction in my design. That part wanted to stay convinced I wasn't with Pete; we were just friends, with benefits. But the me that came out of my senior year, *that* me wanted to call Pete my boyfriend. Wanted to hold him and kiss him and tell him how fucking amazing he was. A war was constantly being fought inside my head, and I couldn't pick a side. The angel and the devil, each fighting for a different me.

"Nothing." Axel glanced behind me, drawing my attention away from him.

Pete was about halfway to us. His hands were in his jacket pockets, the ghostly symbol of his Ghostbusters t-shirt covering his chest. God, he was such a nerd. An adorable, sweet, kindhearted nerd who was screwing himself by wanting to be with me.

"Why don't I get your number, then?" Axel's request took me out of my own pathetic ramblings. "Maybe I'll see you out there."

"You want my number?"

He shrugged. "Sure." Pulling out his phone, he swiped off the current apps before looking back up. "I'll text you, so you have mine."

Knots formed in my stomach, but I welcomed it, like finding an old beat-up doll I used to carry around as a kid. I got some sick pleasure out of this guy jumping at the bit. "Sure." Instead of telling him, I grabbed his phone out of his hand and punched in my number. Placing it back in his hand, the tips of my fingers touched his palm. He was warm, but not sweaty or clammy. Warm like a fire after being out in the cold all day. That kind of warmth.

"Hey." Pete came up behind me. "Food ordered." He nodded to Axel. "Hello again."

"Hey." Axel pushed the button to the side and returned his phone to his pocket. "Heard you were road tripping, too."

Pete nodded. "Yeah. Heading to California."

"What part?"

"Los Angeles. So, the big time, I guess."

"Cool. I'm from Santa Barbara. Not too far from where you're going." With a grin, Axel looked back at me. "I'll text you."

"Nothing inappropriate, I hope."

A breathy laugh escaped him. "How'd you know that's what I was gonna do?" He nodded to Pete. "Nice to see you again, Pete. Maybe we'll see you on the road."

"Yeah, all right." Pete held up his hand as Axel slunk away, his face still beaming. "Later."

I watched him get absorbed into the crowd. A few seconds later, my phone buzzed in my bag. Pulling it free, I switched on my messages and there was Axel, winking at a selfie he must have taken right after he bailed. I turned to face Pete. "He's on a road trip, too. Funny, huh?"

"Yeah," Pete said, tight-lipped. "Hilarious."

I leaned my elbow on my hip. "What's your problem?"

His muscles tensed, arms pressed at his sides. "You gave him your number?"

I shrugged. "Yeah. And?" My phone fell back in my bag as I waited for him to give me a good reason for his attitude.

Okay, I already knew the reason for his attitude. I gave my number out. So what? Whoopty-freaking-do. My plan wasn't to jump the guy's bones or anything. It was innocent. Innocent without meaning to be. Seriously, who was I trying to kid? Only myself.

Of course, Pete seemed a little peeved. He had every right to be. The girl who he wanted to be with just gave her number out to another guy. The girl who denied his request to be a couple.

The legal definition of a user was standing in my shoes. Shit, I was always a user. And I never felt bad about it until now, seeing him standing there, clearly upset that I had done this.

I forced the bad girl out, because if I didn't, I'd fall in his arms and go against the code I'd sworn myself to since embarking on this trip. "I can give my number to whoever I want. You're not in charge of me."

"Fine. Whatever." He took a step back. "Our food is probably waiting for us." With a turn on his sneakers, he walked away.

The devil and the angel were at war on my shoulders. My conscious would never be clean. I was too used to keeping it dirty. Fuck me sometimes.

eight

. . .

minnesota, wednesday, july 22nd

THE TUNNEL of fish was a staple in most aquariums these days, but that didn't make it any less impressive. Water climbed up, over, and down on all sides. Rocks and sea plants I couldn't name littered the white and gray sand that coated the artificial ocean. The blue of the tank made every color of fish stand out like a headlight in the dark. Fish I hadn't known existed swam above the glass, flashing their underbellies, sharks and stingrays gliding overhead.

Putting my hand on the glass, the coolness seeped through my fingers as the fish came to observe me. Pete stood a few feet away, his hands in his jacket pockets, staring at a turtle combing the bottom of the tank. He had said very little when we sat down to eat. I thought the aquarium would get him out of his funk, but my number exchange was obviously still on his mind.

I ran my hand over my naked wrist, feeling the absence of my bracelet more than I normally did. What would my dad think of me at a time like this? As quickly as the thought manifested, it disappeared again. I couldn't allow it to fester. Not now.

With a drawn-out sigh, I dragged my fingers along the glass toward him. Propping myself on the thick wooden banister to deter kids from climbing all over the place, I sat down and nudged him with my shoulder. "You gonna tell me what you're moping around for?"

His eyes shifted behind his glasses, body unmoving. "The reason seems pretty clear to me."

Rolling my eyes upward, I focused on a few swimming fish to keep myself grounded. "I get that you're jealous."

"Is that what you think?" Pete turned and walked to the other side of the tunnel. A few people moved in between us as Pete leaned against the wall before the exit. "Look, you can't make out with me one minute and then grab a guy's number the next. That's not cool."

"Why can't I? Welcome to friends with benefits, Pete." I stood, folding my arms in the strap of my bag, half leaning on the banister. "I didn't plan on it. It just happened."

"Like not telling me you didn't want to be together before we even started this trip. That *just* happened too?"

Low blow.

My skin prickling like it was preparing to pop, the pulse against my temples flaring. "That was shitty, I know. But you also said you were fine with it. The whole no strings attached thing, that wasn't a joke."

"So, you're keeping me around until you find something better? Is that it?"

My mind went blank. There was nothing I could say to that. It wasn't true, but it was at the same time. I didn't know what I was doing. He could have walked away, but he didn't. He stayed, and I let him. I didn't have the balls to tell him the whole truth. Because of fear. The easiest way for me to deal with fear was to ignore it. So, here I was, ignoring it.

My hand shot out and pushed him. "Screw you, Pete."

"No. You're selfish. You're only thinking about yourself." He stepped in closer. "I get you don't want to commit right now, but at least have the decency to acknowledge you're not the only one involved here."

He stormed out of the tunnel, leaving me to stew alone for a few hopeless moments. A slap of reality was something I rarely received. I always lived in my world, one I'd created after my reality abruptly shattered. My pulse was still hot, but my body weighed a hundred pounds more than it had two minutes ago. He wasn't wrong. I was selfish. I learned not to care about anyone else but myself. Because when I did, I got spit in the face.

I didn't want to hurt Pete, not when I really thought about it.

Bringing my hands to my face, I rubbed my eyes and pressed my palms into my cheeks. The angel was winning this one. Yeah, I could choose not to commit, but I had to commit, in some small degree. At least attempt to be a good friend, like he was for me. Even when I pined for more, I had to control it. Be honest. Not a bitch.

I found him sitting on a bench in the middle of the mall, slouching over his phone. He was bouncing his right leg like crazy, which was a clear sign to me that his anxiety hadn't been quenched. The condensation from the drink I purchased for him moistened my fingers. Taking a deep breath to calm the storm roaring in my stomach, I walked up to him and held out the honey-colored beverage. He glanced up at me, bringing his knees together to let me sit.

"Hey." I sat down, moving his precious bubble tea close to him. "I wasn't sure what flavor you wanted."

Pete eyed me for a minute before taking the drink from my hand. Bringing the straw to his mouth, he took a generous sip. Small opaque bubbles shot up the straw, along with the liquid. After he parted from it, he seemed more relaxed, offering me a small yet satisfying smirk.

"Honey tea and tapioca. Thanks."

I flipped my hair back. "Sure thing."

He nudged the drink close to me. "Wanna try?"

"I already stole a sip. I know it's good."

His smile grew, and so did mine. The storm subsided, and it was a little easier to breathe. But the olive branch had yet to be passed completely. Not until I said what I needed to say.

"Look," my gaze dropped to my feet as I swung them just above the floor, "I'm sorry. You're right." I forced myself to look at him. "I was being selfish. And . . . it's not fair to you. As a friend. I can't be like that."

The drink settled in his lap. "I appreciate the apology. Really."

My shoulders came up as I leaned against the bench. "I'm not used to it. So, I'm not gonna be perfect at it."

"I don't expect you to be."

"But I won't hide anything from you. I'll tell you. Straight up. Because," my lips came together as I waited for the yelling inside my head to shut up, "you are important to me, Pete."

His eyes softened. I severely broke out of my comfort zone, but screw it. I had to do something differently. Being free didn't mean being careless. I had to give honesty a chance and quit backstabbing. I had to take the hard road this time. A little selfishness but also selflessness. I'd make this no-strings-attached thing work as best I could, without stomping Pete into the dirt.

My head fell toward him as I leaned against his arm. "Am I forgiven?"

I felt his chest rise as he took a deep breath. "For now."

"What? The bubble tea wasn't enough?"

"Oh, no. I'll think of an official way for you to make it up to me."

I sat up, narrowing my eyes at him. "What makes something official?"

He shrugged, taking another sip from his honey bubble tea. "No idea."

"Hmm, okay." I fell against his arm, throwing my feet up on the bench. He didn't wait to prop his arm to give me ample room, still sipping on his beverage. The air was definitely lighter now that I got that off my chest. Hopefully, I could keep it that way, because as much as we were in this together, a lot more was riding on my ass than his.

But that sinister voice whispered in my ear again, telling me to see what Axel was up to. Ignoring it now was easy. But the temptation would always be there, waiting for me to fail.

nine

. . .

south dakota, thursday, july 30th

WE WERE HEADING to the badlands of South Dakota. The midday sun tried to pierce the thick layer of protection my shades provided. One hand on the wheel, the other casually leaning on the inside of the car door, I stared out at the open road. I had never seen so many mountains in one place. The winding road ran through an endless rock landscape covered in sand. And the road was never straight. It curved and curled like a strand of tread, tight before releasing.

I had my hair up in a bun because it was way too hot to have my mop down. The windows were usually open, but this was an air conditioning kind of ride into uncharted territory. I rolled the sleeves up on my purple flannel, matching the style of my denim Bermudas. Pete sat casually beside me, his seat back and nose in another comic book. I couldn't make out the title from the driver's seat, but there was a mean-looking purple guy and a raccoon with guns blazing on the cover. Or blasters or whatever the sci-fi version of guns were called.

Gremlin lounged in his cat carrier in the back, his scruffy brown face pressed up against the soft mesh, sound asleep. We usually let him hang out in the back freely, but with all the twists in the road, he was more stable in the carrier.

Music, chosen by Pete, played through the radio via Bluetooth, but it was one band I didn't really care too much for.

"Hey." I glanced at him. "Can you change this up? Not really digging it."

Putting the comic upside down in his lap, so he wouldn't lose his place, Pete adjusted his "Ziggy Stardust" zombie shirt and reached for the phone. "What's your poison?" Before I could answer, he held up his hand. "Wait. I have a question for you."

I shrugged. "Shoot."

"What's your guilty pleasure song?"

Shaking my head, I peeked at him with my mouth upturned. "Like . . . a song I indulge in?"

"Secretly indulge in. Like, if anyone found out you loved it, you'd be embarrassed."

"First off, I don't get embarrassed." I leaned back in my seat. "Second, I have a few. But there's one I'd occasionally dance to in my room when I was home alone."

"A secret dance song?" He smiled. "Put it on."

"I can't."

"Why not?"

I glanced at him, glad I had my sunglasses on so he couldn't see my reluctant expression. "It's on my phone and I'm not letting you dig in there to look for it." I placed both hands on the wheel. "If I'm gonna let you listen to it, it needs to be a surprise."

"Fair enough." Pete swiped the screen on his phone to bring it up. "Interested in mine?"

"I don't know. Should I be afraid?"

"Uh, no. It's not that bad."

I smirked. "For you, but I might think less of you for it."

"Well, that is something I'll have to live with then." After a few more seconds of scrolling, Pete gave me that one brow smirk. The sun glinting off his glasses made him seem very sure of himself. "Are you ready?"

"Roll it out."

I waited for the song to kick on after he presumably pressed play. As soon as the 90s style beats kicked off in the car stereo, I practically choked on my breath. My lips sputtered as amusement poured out of me, the opening melody of "Everybody" by the Backstreet Boys was about to explode into hard-hitting boy band bliss. I could barely sit up straight, let alone drive.

"What is so funny?" Pete asked, an ear to ear grin pasted on his face.

My foot eased off the gas so I didn't accidentally crash the car. Taking a deep breath, I held in the last few bouts of laughter, letting them pop off my chest. "Backstreet Boys? You closet fanboy, you. I bet you had a poster on your wall as a kid, too."

His forehead creased, eyes casually rolling upward. "So, what if I did?"

A huff, followed by a soft chuckle, leaked through my teeth. "Wow. What spurred that obsession on?"

"My mom was a huge Backstreet Boys fan when I was little. She'd blast their music all day in the car and at home. It was mind numbing." He shrugged. "But we used to sing along to their songs all the time. Kim and I would try to copy the moves from the music videos. So, it's kind of special, I guess. Brings back memories of simpler times."

Sweet and sentimental. Those two personality traits seemed to go hand in hand. I had to bask in the music for a bit, picturing mini Pete dancing across the kitchen floor with Kimberly in their socks and pjs. It rendered the smile on my face unmovable, thinking about my childhood and how fun it was before everything went to shit.

As the song wound down, I glanced at Pete again, who was mouthing the vocals with strong enthusiasm. Another BSB beat followed closely behind the last few notes. Pete moved to change the track.

"You can leave it on." He looked at me. "I'll let you bask in Backstreet Boy bliss a little longer."

A faint meow came from the carrier in the backseat. Pete looked behind the seat. "Almost there, little guy. Hang in there."

I glanced in the rearview mirror. There were no cars behind us, just dead, open road. A sign for the Sage Creek Campground came up on our right. Two miles and we'd be able to park the car, stretch our legs, and chill.

"Hey," Pete pointed ahead, "is that it?"

A large strip of road cut out of the plains 2 miles out, leading down to what appeared to be an open circle of cars, tents, and small RVs scattered about.

I took the exit right and drove down the dirt road. "We're home." I turned the car right as the tires cracked along the dirt. A small kiosk sat a few feet away, and I pulled the car up to the window. A woman with short brown hair, wearing hiking boots, smiled up at the window as I rolled it down.

"Hey there." She beamed. "Welcome to Sage Creek."

"We have a spot here," I said, stripping off my sunglasses.

"What's your name, sweetie?"

"Carter. Ashley."

The woman ducked back into her booth. Pete poked my arm, catching my attention. "She called you sweetie."

I scoffed enthusiastically. "Clearly she doesn't know me."

The woman came back, returning to her spot by the window, leaning against it.

"Got you right here." She stretched out her finger at the large wagon train circle. "All cars bear right. Your spot is the one just before the curve on the end. Number 8."

"Thank you." Pete waved.

"Your site has a wooden awning and picnic table for your use. No running water here. So, I hope you brought plenty."

"Oh, we're prepared." Pete smiled. "Got our porta-potty and everything."

The woman came off from the window. "Enjoy your stay. And no feeding the buffalo. They come through here often."

Both Pete and I waved as I eased back on the gas pedal. The road was bumpy, making me glad we had the Subaru. Gremlin was really bouncing around in his carrier now, meowing like crazy as we came around the first turn. There were a few residents already assembled at their designated sites. They waved as we passed.

"Geez, this is the middle of nowhere." The flat, sand-toned grass left him slack jawed.

"It's a far cry from New York, that's for sure."

Pete turned to me. "We'll be like Indiana Jones searching for the Ark. Can we do it?"

"Hell yeah, we can."

We pulled into our spot, right on the side of the circle. I turned the wheel all the way to the left and backed the camper a few feet from the picnic table. Pete shot out of the car like a bullet, ready to get his Airwalks dirty on the prairie. Unbuckling my seatbelt, I killed the engine.

I stared out into the openness. This place reminded me of my dad. It could be because he always talked about places like this, large open land that stretched on for miles and miles without an end. The stories he'd tell me about him growing up in a place that wasn't here. A place that seemed like a fairyland away from the United States.

"Hey." Pete's calm voice chimed in from the window. Looking at him, I forced a smile.

"Hi."

He twisted his mouth, his head leaning to one side. "Something wrong?"

I shook my head. "No. It's just." Looking down at my fumbling hands, I took a deep breath and let it out harshly. "This place reminds me of my dad."

"Yeah?" He looked out across the sand-soaked grass.

I joined him in his silence for a moment, just letting the quiet, windless day suffocate my senses. "He used to tell me stories of places like this. Where he grew up."

"Where was that?"

"Australia."

"Wow, Australia?"

I nodded without blinking or drawing myself away from nature. "He grew up in the outback, far from Sydney, or anything resembling civilization. The shit he used to tell me he did as a kid. I thought Australia was in another galaxy. Some magical place he'd take me to one day."

"Did he?"

A knot tightened in my throat. My eyes found him watching me quietly. I had his full attention. A sudden urge to push him away pulled at my arms, but I held it down. "No," I whispered.

Pete slowly placed his hand on my shoulder. It immediately dissolved the need to run. "I hope this is the next best thing. And who knows? Maybe one day we'll go there."

It wasn't his words that eased me out of my funk; it was his touch. He cared. Genuinely and whole-heartedly. He could have said anything and it wouldn't have mattered. I reached for his hand and took it, squeezing it into my palm. Jerk. He had no business making me feel cared for.

Pete popped the door handle and slipped away as he opened my door. "Ready to explore the shit out of this place?"

Holding out his hand to me, I didn't think I could smile any wider. I took it without question, letting him pull me out of my seat, crashing against him like a wave on a rock. His arm came around me and we looked at each other, waiting for something to happen. Placing a careful hand on his chest, I threw my head over my shoulder, raising my brow to copy the still-unabated joy I had plastered across my face.

A sweet meow squeaked from inside the car. "We should probably feed Gremlin first before he goes agro on us."

"You're probably right." A careful swipe of his hand pulled some loose springs of hair behind my ear. Despite the dry rolling heat, his fingers tickled my skin like droplets of cold water. For a second, I'd forgotten the doubts I'd been feeding myself to justify any decisions I'd made about him. All that mattered right now was him.

ten

. . .

south dakota, friday, july 31st

I COULD SEE the sunset from any direction. We used our picnic table to enjoy a chicken and cheese quesadilla dinner. Our camper used solar energy, so we could run the stove and microwave without plug-in electricity. I dragged the sponge across the only steel pot we brought on this trip, letting the soap bubble to remove the remnants of sauce from its surface. We boiled some water for washing, letting it drain into our mini sink.

The Bluetooth speakers were busting out tunes low enough so we wouldn't disturb any of our fellow campers. I shook the remaining water off the pot, placing it on a towel beside the sink to allow it to dry. Pete had just collected the last of our disposable plates into a black garbage bag. Walking over to the kitchenette, he opened one of the three small drawers and popped the bag in the white waste bin we kept there.

"All cleaned up." He slapped his hands together and looked at me. "Can I get in there?"

With a nod, I scooted over for him to get to the sink. He grabbed the bottle of soap and lathered his hands before pumping on the water to wash up. I waited, standing close enough to him so our arms were barely touching. Every brush of skin on skin made the rainfall all over my senses again, relieving me of everything that had been weighing me down.

My phone buzzed in my pocket. Taking a step back, I pulled it out to see Axel's smirking face pop up on my screen. I swiped to my messages.

AXEL

Made it to North D. You two have a safe drive to wherever it is you're goin'?

"Whose that?" Pete asked, wiping his hands on a towel.

"Axel," I answered without hesitation. "They're in North Dakota."

"You sure he isn't behind one of these mountains or something?"

Looking at Pete, a squint of my eyes painted a smirk on his face. "He better not be."

I looked back at my phone.

We're south of you. Roughing it out in the badlands.

A ping of a return text didn't even give me a chance to look up.

Perfect place for a harpy like you.

Don't be a smartass. Go to bed.

Can't. Night skiings a-callin. Later, Harpy.

Watch out for trees.

Looking up from my phone, I noticed Pete wasn't near me anymore. He was back at the picnic table, sitting with his back to me, staring up at the darkening sky. Stars were already making themselves known against the fading light. Clasping my hands behind my back, I strolled to him on the bench. He didn't acknowledge I was there, keeping himself locked on the emerging stars. I followed his gaze, watching more and more appear in the sky every minute.

"We'll probably see a ton tonight." I swung my legs back and forth on the bench.

"Yeah," Pete replied rather dully. "Probably."

Skidding my heels across the ground, I bumped my knees together. His hands rested on the bench, fingers splayed across the well-sanded wood. I slowly crept my fingers into his to get some sort of reaction out of him. The Axel thing was still bothering him. I promised I wouldn't keep any secrets, but he would have to learn to get over this hump on his own.

I leaned on him, forcing my head into his line of sight. "Hey." With my free hand, I pulled out my phone and waved it to grab more of his attention. "Wanna hear my guilty pleasure song?"

Pete's eyes moved from me to my phone, then back to the sky. "You don't have to if you don't want to."

"No. I do. And it's only fair." I stood up. "I mean, you confessed you're a closet boy band junkie."

Leaning my hand on my hip, I waited for his answer. His face was placid. Brown eyes from behind his glasses concentrated but swimming with sadness. I hated seeing him so down, even if the reason was juvenile.

"I'm gonna play it whether or not you want me to." I clicked on my music app and scrolled through, landing on the song that brought back the happiest of memories.

The Bluetooth player skipped as it kicked on the tune. The tambourine rattled to life as The Crystal's sweet vocals sang "Then He Kissed Me". I couldn't help but move my body to the music, letting the lyrics pour out of me without shame or embarrassment. Spinning around, I rolled my shoulders back, swinging my hips to the beat.

The second part of the song came on. Looking over at Pete, he had a half smile on his face as he watched me strike a pose here and there and everywhere. Not wasting another minute, I skipped, grabbing his arm to tug him to his feet.

"My parents would dance to this song all the time," I said, as I dragged him away from the table. "Now, it's our turn."

I put his arms around me as I clasped mine behind his neck. He didn't want to move, but my continued singing only made that half smile into a whole one. As the song continued, he loosened up, keeping his hands firmly around me. His grin turned into a relieving chuckle. I leaned back, forcing him to spin me around. Coming back up, his arm rose to my back, holding me closer to him as light laughter carried us through the music.

I giggled, my hands coming to rest on his chest, feeling his heart beat uncontrollably. My voice dropped to a whisper as our dancing ceased to just the two of us standing there in the flickering starlight.

Pete tucked his chin, touching his forehead to mine as I breathed out the next line of the song. "I felt so happy I almost cried . . . "

It took little coaxing for my lips to reach for his. My hand came to the back of his neck, keeping him there to prolong the inevitable. The chills were popping on my skin like bubbles filled with too much air. But as soon as it started, it ended.

Pete pulled away, huffing loudly toward the ground. "Sorry," he said, as his arms fell from me. "I can't do this."

He turned on his heels and made his way back to the camper. My heart jumped into my throat as I launched myself after him. Panic multiplied in my mind like a hundred reproducing rabbits. If I couldn't catch him, he'd never come back.

"Wait." I grabbed his arm right outside the camper door.

Lifting his head upward, he turned to face me as his tongue dragged across his tight upper lip. "What?"

I dropped his arm. "Can you just wait, please?"

He shrugged, shaking his head. "Wait for what?" His chin dropped as his hands ran through his dirty blond hair. "I don't know what you want. I . . . don't even know what we're doing half the time."

My mouth fell open. "We're just . . . here."

"Are you? Because I know I am. All of me. I'm here. You," his eyes rolled up to the sky, "you're on another planet." He looked back at me. "You're the worst of John Bender, and Claire, rolled up into one."

I swallowed hard at the Breakfast Club comparison, trying desperately to keep the heat bubbling inside my stomach from exploding. "You think I know what the *hell* I'm doing?"

"Well, I'd hoped you'd had some idea."

"Pete." I had to close my eyes and take a deep breath. "I'm a chicken with my fucking head cut off."

"So, what does that mean, then? Because I don't know where the hell I fit into your shit! *Any of it.*"

"It's not that simple."

"Nothing ever is with you." His back hit the camper. Leaning against it, Pete crossed his arms and watched me, waiting for an answer that would satisfy him. I didn't have one. Because I didn't know the answer. This was a toss-up. Everything. All of it. I didn't know what went up first and what came down last. One day I'd be happy and ready to commit, and the next, I wanted to run with my tail between my legs. He didn't know how much of a coward I was. The trap held me captive and I couldn't escape.

I didn't want him to feel unwanted or used, but that part of me—that manipulator—wouldn't go away. Like an annoying friend you wanted to punch in the face, but couldn't bring yourself to do it. In the past, I wanted to make anyone who even thought of caring about me miserable, so I felt important. There was never a time I challenged it so much. I wasn't strong enough yet to overcome it. It was stronger than I was. Maybe it always would be.

Pressing my lips together, I tucked my hands under my arms and approached him. "I'm scared, okay?" He didn't say a word, so I didn't stop. "You terrify me. The whole 'us' thing?" I could feel my eyes swell with tears. "I don't know how to handle it. It was different before because it was so new and I was . . . lost in the tides of it. Now . . . " I sucked air into my nostrils to stifle my emotions. " . . . I can't keep my head above water. I can't get over the fear of drowning. The pressure. I've done it before." Holding my breath, I shut my eyes. "It never gets better."

Everything froze, but not the refreshing cold that Pete gave me whenever he touched my sun-soaked skin. I was icy, like some unloved puppy left in a cardboard box in the rain. Waiting and wanting. Always wanting.

I'm pathetic.

I ran my hand up and down my arm, stopping at my wrist, remembering the pain from the past four years of my life before Pete. I hated it. Hated remembering that even though I tore my bracelet off my body, it was still there, sitting in a little keepsake box above the bed of the camper. Part of me wanted to feel it hanging from me like an anvil and part of me was afraid to even think of looking at it again. It's colorful knitting, symbolizing the death of my father and the birth of my spiraling life.

A light touch ran across my cheek to catch a stray tear. I came back into focus upon the one guy who'd offered me so much.

"Look." I grasped his arm as I batted away my sadness as best I could. "I felt different today. Like this is all I could ever want. I can't promise you it will always be this way. That I won't run again. That I won't push. That I won't fuck it all up. But I'm trying. I'm really trying."

A calm exhale deflated the tension on Pete's face. "I'm trying too."

"I can't promise you anything until I figure myself out."

A spark spread across his face. He looked at me with a smirk, which I couldn't help but mirror. "Believe me, I never thought it would be easy." His lips pressed together as he took a breath. "So, what do you want? Right now."

My heart picked up like a speeding bullet in the dark. I wanted him, all of him. It was selfish of me to ask for it, to even think about it. But I wanted to get lost in his watermelon taste. Keep my arms wrapped around him and ask him to never let me go. I wanted to forget how terrified I was of taking the leap, to just jump. Maybe I'd try to climb out once I hit the ground, but I didn't want to think of what would happen afterward.

He was it. Right now. I wanted to feel him until the sun came up and maybe even after that.

Squeezing his arm, I inched closer to him. The proximity spinning my stomach into a merry-go-round gone haywire. "That depends on you."

His hand slid across my collarbone, coming to rest at the base of my neckline. "I don't wanna screw things up."

"That's impossible," I whispered as he held me against him, our pulses practically in sync. "Everything you've done, it's only made things better. Harder, but better." My teeth bit the inside of my lip. "I don't want you to think."

"All right." Our foreheads came together, his sweet summer scent brushing against my cheek. "Then I won't."

He hit me like a wave, crashing against me with movable force. Wrapping my arms around his neck, I pulled him into me, never wanting him to break us apart again. His hands glided across my back, coming up my shirt to rake my skin. It was electrifying. I jumped against him, his arms catching me as I wrapped my legs around his waist.

He turned with me in his arms and our tongues down each other's throats. Pressing me against the camper, he fumbled for the door handle. It wasn't a successful attempt. Stifling a laugh, I broke away from him momentarily and tried to help. "Wait. Let me get . . . wait!"

Airy elation escaped us both as we finally pried it open. I fell against the bed, crawling backward so he had room to get in. Kicking off my sandals, Pete rid himself of his sneakers before shutting the door.

He climbed over and I fell against the bed as his arm came around me. "We don't have to do this if you don't want to."

So sincere. What the hell was I doing? Who cared? If I deserved him or not, it didn't matter.

"Shut up and come here."

I dragged him in with a kiss, letting his hands draw up my sides, loosening my halter as I pulled his shirt up his back. He sat up and finished my handiwork, and I did the same. Coming together in the center of the bed, we kissed. His toned muscles were all over my terra cotta skin.

"Wait." I carefully peeled off his glasses and placed them on the shelf above the bed. His smile, both hungry and filled with so much care. Pulling my hair free from my hair tie, it tickled the top of my shoulders as Pete came in for another steal.

Now would be it, the moment I'd let myself be his. And give him everything he could ever want.

eleven

. . .

south dakota, friday, july 31st

I ROLLED over in the bed, pulling the soft sheet over my shoulders. Pete lay with his eyes closed, his hand resting on his bare chest, rising and falling with every steady breath. I inched closer to him, nuzzling his shoulder and lacing my arm over him. One eye popped open, a smirk cast across his face. "Hey."

"Don't mind me," I said, looking at him with dreamy eyes. He leaned a few centimeters forward and touched his nose to mine, drawing me in for another soft, satisfying kiss.

"So," I whispered. "How was your first rodeo?"

He slid back, his smile breaking into a breathy laugh. "Hold on a sec. You thought I was a virgin?"

"Well . . . yeah."

Pete rolled his head back, bringing his hand to rest on his forehead. "Oh, my God. How did this never come up?" His enthusiasm returned to meet me. "I'm not a virgin, Ash. Haven't been since junior year."

It didn't happen often, but I could feel blood rush to my face.

There was no reason for me to assume that he was, but I guessed part of me wanted to hold the honor.

"Are you embarrassed?" His arms came around me playfully.

"No. I don't get embarrassed." I tried to roll out of his arms. But he kept me there.

Pulling me into his chest, he buried his face in my locks against my neck. "You are so embarrassed."

"Shut up, Pete." I tried to look annoyed, but it was impossible. Instead, I drove my hand against his chest and let a short giggle escape.

"It's okay, if you thought that. I mean, was I good? For a pretend virgin?"

My mouth upturned, observing him in judgment. Hard to lie about something like this. With Wes, it was always heavy, like we were slowly cooking inside a furnace. But with Pete . . . I wasn't suffocating.

He was smooth, like a charming man. There was raw emotion involved, and when that mixed with the physical, it was bliss. Like surrendering your body to the tides of the sea. A place I could get lost in forever.

"I'll never admit how good or bad you were." Our noses touched again, the elation never leaving me.

"Wanna do it again?" He loosened his hold on me, but kept me close enough to get lost in his summer scent.

I dragged my fingers through his hair, tickling behind his ears. "Don't you need a break?"

"Are you trying to convince me or yourself?"

I pulled my leg over him, feeling our nakedness between the sheets. Oh, he could go again. "Clearly, you don't know me well enough."

"Oh, really?" He glanced toward the shelf above the bed. "How many condoms do you have stashed up there?"

I dragged my fingers up his arms toward his neck. "Enough for one more round."

We didn't waste time getting right back to kissing and raising our blood pressure. His flavor was addicting. His hand dragging through my hair as his lean-muscled chest crashed against my frame. If Edison needed a lesson on how to make electricity, this would be it. He was good, so fucking good. Every touch, every tingle, every attempt to come together like dough was pure and exhilarating. I hated how perfect he was, in every way, shape, and form.

It couldn't have been more than a few seconds, but someone bellowed from outside our camper so loud that it distracted me. Pulling away reluctantly, both of us leaned up toward the closed window.

"What the hell?" Pete crawled a little closer to get a better look.

Holding the surrounding sheet, I lingered as the shouting continued. "Who is that?"

Gremlin slunk to me, plopping in my lap with his tail up and purring in full force. Getting himself to the edge of the bed, Pete pulled on his boxers and shirt. As he was getting in his shorts, I slid over to the window to grab a peek.

There were a few people toward the center of the campground. A man with medium length hair and a square face was arguing with two others who were trying to restrain him. He was thrashing to escape their grip, pointing toward our spot. Following his finger, the picnic table at our site came into view.

A girl was sitting there. Her jet black hair hanging in her face, hands grasping the bench beneath her. She wore red plaid pajama pants and a plain black t-shirt that was a little big on her.

"I'm going out there." Pete pulled on the door handle.

"Wait." I hurried over to him, grabbing my clothes that lay scattered on the bed. "I'm coming too."

It only took me a few seconds to be decent, and the two of us exited the camper. The girl stood as we approached. Her dark almond eyes were puffy and her brows drawn up in surprise. Wetness from crying still clung to her copper-toned skin.

"I'm sorry." She sniffed and backed away. "I didn't mean to bother you."

"No. It's cool." Pete and I walked over to the table. The girl shied away, but the screaming man's voice stung our ears, forcing us all to look in his direction.

He barreled toward us, free of the two men who were holding him back, hair disheveled and feet incapable of walking straight. His appearance suggested that he was related to this girl somehow. Same jet black hair and copper skin, even the same eyes.

"You can't leave, Zitkala!" he hollered, shaking a wobbly hand toward the girl. He then spoke in a language I never had the pleasure of hearing before. But, judging from what cinema portrayed, it was some Native American dialect.

The other two men grabbed him again. An enormous guy with white hair pulled him down to the ground to sit. "Now, you settle down, you hear? We already called the police on ya."

"Fuck you!" The drunk blathered on in his language.

A few others stood outside their tents and campers, watching the entire scene unfold. I looked at the girl he had called Zitkala. She folded her arms against her chest, tears streaming down her face. I placed a comforting arm around her shoulders. She tensed at first, but then leaned against me, letting the rest of her sadness fall on my bare arms.

The drunk yelled again, calling her names like a madman.

I came around to face her, taking her by the shoulders. "Do you know that man?" I asked her calmly.

Zitkala nodded. "He's my dad."

Red and blue flashing lights came into focus, sailing into the center of the campground. We watched two cops get out of the car and move toward her father and the other men restraining him.

"Come on," one cop said, "on your feet." They dragged him up.

"Kala! Kala! Damn you, fucking badges. *Zitkala!*"

"Take it easy, take it easy," the cops spoke calmly, trying to bring Zitkala's father down from his drunken stupor. After a few minutes, he seemed more civilized.

"Had a little too much to drink tonight?"

We sat and watched from the picnic table. Pushing the damp hair out of her eyes, Kala's gaze darted from the police to me. "I should go over there."

Her chest rose and dropped. Sadness strained her eyelids and tightened her chin, despite her trying to garner some composure.

Pete leaned over my shoulder, placing a supportive hand on my back. "You sure?"

"Yeah." She sniffed as she stood. "Sorry to bother you."

The younger and more trim of the two cops walked over toward us. Zitkala swallowed before meeting him halfway.

"Are you Zitkala?" he asked.

She nodded. "Yes. I'm his daughter."

"And how old are you?"

"17."

It took everything in me not to run out there and pull this girl away from this entire situation. My mind immediately started flipping through the slides of my relationship with Wes. I couldn't count the number of times the cops were at his house because his dad was stone drunk. He'd broken more than just a few windows. He and Wes were beating each other so badly one night, I hid in the cabinet under the sink, crying on the phone to the 911 dispatcher to hurry before someone ended up dead.

"Your dad is in awful shape. Anyone around you could call?"

She shook her head; her face firm to keep from letting any emotion show.

"We can take him in, put him in a holding cell for a night—"

"No, he'll be okay. We just got into a fight. That's all."

The cop clicked his pen against his pad. "Did he put his hands on you?"

Kala's lips pressed together as she shook her head. "No."

The cop glanced at us before gesturing Kala to follow him to where his partner and her dad were still standing.

"Shit." Pete sighed, now sitting on the bench next to me. "Think she'll be okay?"

I looked at him, my fists balled against my lap. "No. I don't." I watched the altercation slowly wind down in conversation between the cops and Zitkala. After a few more minutes, one cop gave Kala a card before getting back into their cruiser. The other took her drunken father by the arm, leading them back toward an RV about seven sites to the left of us. Zitkala walked close behind them. About halfway, the cop gave her father's arm to her and they proceeded to the RV alone.

We sat in silence as the cop returned to their car. A few minutes later, they peeled away toward the single road leading out of the grounds. My attention turned back to the RV where Zitkala and her father had disappeared into.

"Come on." I pulled Pete's arm as I stood.

"What?" Pete followed me across the wagon circle. "What exactly are we doing?"

"Making sure she's okay."

"And this is a good idea because . . . "

I raised my brow at him. "Where are your hero instincts with this one, huh?"

Pete sighed. "Fair enough."

We walked across the campground, and I knocked a few times on her door. Pete stood right beside me. A few seconds later, it opened a crack. Zitkala peered out, looking us over with a furrowed brow. "Yes?"

"Hey," I said. "We wanted to make sure you were okay."

Zitkala glanced behind her. "Hold on a second." The door closed, then opened fully. She stepped down the two stairs to meet us outside, closing the door behind her. She wrapped a blanket around her shoulders, pulling it close to hide anything she might not want others to see.

"Look, I'm sorry I bothered you—"

"It's okay. We're not mad about it or anything. I'm Ashley, by the way." I looked over at Pete.

"I'm Pete."

She gave a weak smile. "I'm Kala."

Pete eyed the door. "So, your dad. Is he . . . "

"He passed out." She brushed her straight hair away from her face. "He'll be fine."

"And what about you?" I asked.

Kala blinked a handful of times before she tightened her jaw. Her posture shifted, hands pulling the blanket more securely around her. "I'll be fine."

"Hey." Pete nodded toward our site. "If you need someplace to get away while you're here, come on by. Maybe have breakfast with us tomorrow?"

"Oh, I don't know."

"What could it hurt?" He shrugged. "I promise we aren't creeps."

A flash of a smile twitched at the corner of her lips. "I didn't think you were creeps."

I tilted my head to the right and raised an expecting brow. "So. Breakfast. Our place tomorrow morning? Like nine-ish?"

She lowered her chin as her eyes darted from me to Pete, like she was trying to figure out if we were being genuine or if there was some ulterior motive behind all this.

There was a lot she wasn't saying, but I couldn't just forget what we saw. I knew what it was like being alone to pick up the pieces of someone else's broken life. I would never wish that on another person.

That's how Pete unofficially caught my attention over six months ago. A stranger, minding his own business, caught me and Wes in one of our many intolerable spats. He didn't care who I was or the target he had willingly painted on his back from stepping between me and Wes. Someone was in trouble and he acted because it was the right thing to do.

This was no different.

"All right," she finally said, raising her head with a weak smile. "Sounds good."

twelve

· · ·

south dakota, saturday, august 1st

SHOVING the scrambled eggs into my mouth, my eyes dropped to my copy of *No Fear Shakespeare*. I was halfway through *Macbeth*, enjoying one of his wife's many maddening rants. It's crazy how, even back in Shakespeare's days, naivety and cynicism still ran rampant for anyone under the age of 21. It just went to show that, even though times change, human beings still go through the same shit.

Pete shuffled over with his paper plate jam-packed with food. He hadn't brushed his hair yet, and it stuck out in a few odd directions. Sausages and eggs with a splash of ketchup and a bottle of orange juice under his arm. He sat down across from me and didn't waste any time enjoying his breakfast.

Twirling my fork in some eggs, I pulled my leg on the bench and leaned my arm across my knee. "You sleep okay?"

"Yeah." He shrugged. "Mostly."

Some more eggs made it into my mouth. "Hope she shows up."

Pete returned to his meal, and I watched him. My dad was a lot like him. Funny. Cheesy. Understanding. And had a hell of a smile. There wasn't anyone I could talk to like I could with my dad. There was shit

I told him and no one else, not Dimitri or Mom, or even Amber. I couldn't explain how Pete made me feel the same way. It felt like betrayal. Because that was my thing with my dad. No one else even came close. Not even in the beginning with Wes.

Swirling my tongue across my gums, I put my plastic fork down on my plate. "Thanks, by the way."

Pete took a long swig of OJ, smacking his lips together in satisfaction. "For what?"

"For backing me up last night."

His arms folded across the edge of the picnic table. "What makes you think I wouldn't have?"

"I don't know. Just . . . expectations from experiences, I guess."

"I see." He stabbed another chunk of sausage. "Don't you know there is no 'I' in *team*?"

Pushing a loose strand of hair out of my face, I came off my knee. "We're a team now?"

"Well, yeah." He swallowed and gestured his fork at me. "I got your back. You have mine."

Did he really believe that? *He's got to be joking*, the snickering voice in my head said, *what a fool*. While the angel swooned and swelled with an extraordinary feeling only falling in love could bring. And here I was, caught in the middle. One was ready to love him for the rest of my life and the other, ready to bury him so deep he would never see the sun again.

Because it was impossible to respond with any ounce of truth, I shoved more eggs in my mouth and leaned my elbow on the table. "Do teammates usually have sex with each other?"

A light breath escaped from his lips. "Only the best kind." His eyes dropped to his plate, moving his food around like he wasn't sure what to do next. "I know you don't want us to be . . . us . . . right now." He looked at me. I swear, the way his eyes shifted with shy intensity shoved an ice pick through my lungs. "But I don't take what we did lightly. It meant something to me."

Fuck emotions. Fuck the ability to feel. Why couldn't we be like animals and just mate to reproduce? The end. No commitment, no one getting hurt. I know some animals mate for life. Wolves, swans, bald eagles, seahorses; they are all the animals that symbolize loyalty, strength, and grace. I was none of those things. But I couldn't unfeel what I felt with him. I wish it was just us fooling around, no strings attached. No strings. What was wrong with me? There were so many strings. I couldn't run a scissor through them fast enough.

"I figured." I sighed, trying to shake off my discomfort by listening to my heart pound loudly in my ribcage. "It did . . . mean something."

His eyes flashed with surprise as my words penetrated his eardrums. Why was this so impossible? The more I allowed myself to be honest, the more it hurt to get the honesty out. The bad still loomed over the good, muscles flexed and ready. I was trying. Trying so hard it killed me to think about it. Nothing would ever be easy with him. Always teeming with uneven rocks to climb and gashes on my knees. If I ever reached the top, I'd be a bloody, sweaty mess, too weak to even want to look out onto the horizon.

Pete's gaze inched past me. "Our guest has arrived."

I turned to see Kala entering our campsite, her arms crossed as she looked over at the kitchenette. She was wearing a loose fitted tee and dark sweatpants. Her hair was tied up in a ponytail and her eyes branded with dark circles.

"Hey!" Pete waved and stood. "Are you hungry?"

Kala darted her eyes to us, tucking her chin like a mouse backed into a corner. Hopping over to her, Pete let out his welcoming grin. "I can make you some eggs. Scrambled?"

"Sure. Thank you." Kala managed a weak smile, but her shyness was clearly a barrier she had yet to break through.

"Go sit with Ash. I'll bring it over to you."

Kala looked at me as I waved her over. Placing her hands over the table, she slid onto the bench before folding her arms again. She wouldn't look up, eyes scanning the wooden surface like she was deciphering a secret message. I would not press her to talk if she didn't feel like it. *Macbeth* fell back into my hand and I resumed my journey into Shakespearean literature. It didn't take long for Kala to drag herself up with curiosity.

"What are you reading?" she asked timidly.

Flipping the book closed on my finger so I wouldn't lose my spot, I turned it around so she could see the cover.

"Oh," she said. "I've never read Shakespeare before."

"He's definitely an acquired taste." I reopened the book. "If you like misery and unhappy endings, he's worth a try." I attempted to continue my journey through the story of this lovely tragedy, but I could sense that our brief talk had helped her relax. Twisting my mouth, I folded the corner of the book, because I didn't own a bookmark, and closed it beside me. "What books do you like to read?"

Kala shrugged, rolling her tongue along the inside of her mouth. "I don't know. I read a lot of fantasy, I guess."

"Like, Harry Potter?" I asked.

"Yeah, I've read those. But I like the epic stuff. Like Tolkien and Jordan's novels. I've read all of Tolkien's books and the ones his son wrote. And I'm almost done with Jordan's *Wheel of Time* series."

"So, that's like books with elves and stuff like that? Magic and sword fighting?"

She nodded. "Yeah. You ever see the *Lord of the Rings* films?"

"Can't say that I have. I don't know if I'd dig it."

"Oh. Well, what things do you like, other than Shakespeare?"

I raised my leg and rested it on the bench. "I like Kung Fu. Bruce Lee was on my TV constantly as a kid. My brothers worshiped him."

"Who was on your TV?" Pete slid a paper plate stacked with scrambled eggs, bacon, and sausage over to Kala. Her eyes widened at the sight of so much food. A small bottle of orange juice was delivered next, before Pete took a seat on my side of the table.

"Thank you." Kala gingerly took the plastic fork in her hand and pushed around the steamy, eggy goodness.

"I was talking about Bruce Lee," I informed Pete. "Kung Fu being a favorite pastime of mine and my brothers growing up."

"Ever see any Tony Jaa films?" Pete asked, clearly excited that I mentioned my good taste in films.

"Hell yeah, *Ong-Bak!* I've seen every single one."

"You continue to impress me." He looked at me with admiration pouring from his eyes. It both disgusted and paralyzed me with how much deeper this was becoming. Hanging my head over my right shoulder, I mustered up a smirk, preparing to fall into yet another daydream.

"Excuse me." Kala's small voice pulled us both out of our sappy romance. "I just wanted to say thanks for inviting me over."

"You were in an unpleasant situation." I looked at her, sliding closer to Pete to rest my knee on his lap. "I know what that's like. Just trying to do the right thing. Plus," I glanced at Pete, "this guy's a professional hero. You couldn't beat it out of him if you tried."

"Oh, trust me. I know at least one person who's tried." Pete smirked.

Kala watched us with silent anticipation. The explanation lacked a lot of pizzazz, but it wasn't more complicated than that. I don't blame her for thinking there might be an ulterior motive. There were a hundred and one reasons I could think of not to trust someone.

Noticing the air had not been cleared, Pete settled his hands on the table.

"We're from New York. Just graduated high school and taking a road trip across the country. We plan on spending the winter in California with her brother. He goes to UCLA and has an apartment there."

Kala nodded, piercing a piece of sausage with her plastic fork. "My mom lives in California. Just outside there."

"Nice." There were a few seconds of silence. "Are you close with your mom? If it's not too personal, I mean."

"Oh, no. It's . . . " Kala pressed her lips and lost eye contact with us. "She's great. I just . . . I stayed with my dad after they got divorced. I couldn't leave him." She shoved her fork in her mouth. "I'm all he has."

That familiar sting twisted my stomach into multiple knots as I watched her resume eating her breakfast. If I didn't know better, I was looking in a mirror from 10 months ago. The same excuses for similar situations. She was trying to save her father, just like I had tried to save Wes. How could you abandon someone you'd revolved your entire world around? I didn't know how close Kala was with her father, but from her determination to not leave his side, I could tell she felt like she was his only hope.

"Thanks for being cool and not some . . . weird fetish couple or something . . . " A shy smile spread across her face, but she tucked it toward her plate to continue eating her breakfast.

Pete's hand met my back. It traveled slowly up and down my spine, setting off those sparks of desire. "I'll go wash up the dishes." Sliding off the bench, he kissed my forehead before making his way to the camper as I tried to refocus on the words of Shakespeare.

No amount of passion-filled rants and terrible nightmares could distract me from reliving those memories of waiting outside Wes' bedroom door for him to stop throwing shit. Or when I'd sit on the curb with tears in my eyes as he peeled away in his car to another street race. Or helping him dump his dad's alcohol down the drain, only to have him come home and beat the piss out of Wes right in front of me.

My parents weren't alcoholics, but I might as well be a victim of one. And of a son who didn't want to change for anyone, not even me.

I'd make sure Kala didn't fall into the same trap I did. No fucking way.

thirteen

. . .

south dakota, sunday, august 2nd

IT WAS another dry day in South D. The scorching sun penetrated the windshield of our Subaru as Pete and I started getting ready to visit the Wind Cave National Park. It would be a bit of a drive, so we were making an early getaway. Pete emerged from the camper, locking the door to protect our precious cargo. And by precious cargo, I meant Gremlin.

I lifted my shades onto the top of my head as I leaned against the car on the passenger's side. My skin was practically shining rusty gold from all the sunscreen I sprayed along my arms, legs, and neck. Pete wore a rather plain gray tank and dark tan cargo shorts. His hair was wet and slicked to one side. A few sparkles of water speckled his glasses. But the sun would suck those up in a heartbeat. His arms flexed as he leaned them over the top of the car to garner my attention. But he didn't need to do anything special. I was already eating him up with my eyes.

"You got the water bottles and the compass?"

"Yes, Dr. Jones." I smirked at his Indiana Jones level of

preparedness. "We're going to a national park, not some unexplored cavern or desert."

"You'll be thanking me when we get lost and have no cell service."

I glanced beyond him to Kala's RV. She was walking around in the front, hanging up what looked like towels along a makeshift line she had set up under the RV canopy. "Why don't we see if Kala wants to come with us?"

Pete raised a brow and glanced over his shoulder. "Yeah?" He looked back at me. "I thought you wanted it to be just us."

"Why? So I can jump your bones in some dark corner of the wind cave?"

"You said it." He smirked. "Not me."

I gestured toward Kala's RV. "Invite her, you sex-crazed maniac."

"So, 'you' means you, right?" His arms came off the car. "Because *I* certainly am *not* a sex-crazed maniac."

I squinted with a scoff. "Get over there!"

Pete raised his hands in defense. "All right. All right." He stepped away from the car. I leaned my chin on my arms as I watched him make his way across the campground. My phone vibrated at my hip. Moving my sunglasses back against my nose, I grabbed it and swiped to see a message notification.

AXEL

Harpy. Check it out.

He sent a picture of him standing with his sunglasses on and his head tilted up like some gangster, on some sort of high platform with an epic landscape behind him. Hanging in the cloud-streaked sky looked like an eagle, soaring through the air with wings spread and eyes fixed on the ground below.

Made a new friend?

You have the same eyes.

I scoffed to myself.

I hope that was a joke. For your sake.

Did I strike a nerve?

I smirked, turning around to lean my back against the car.

Quit being a smartass.

I looked up and saw Pete and Kala chatting it up by her RV still. Something she said made Pete laugh, which made Kala immediately look away with a sheepish grin on her face. He stepped toward her and leaned in a little, saying something. I knew he wasn't flirting, but something about his closeness to her raised the hairs on my neck. She then nodded and moseyed back into the RV, prompting Pete to step out from the canopy and shove his hands in his pockets. He looked back at me and gave a thumbs up.

Mission successful.

Another ding on my phone quickly drew my attention back to the screen and away from my totally unlikely thoughts.

AXEL

You like that I'm a smartass.

I drew my tongue to part my lips. He was right. I did like it. I liked he was Wes before things turned to shit. Wes was flirty in a dangerous sort of way. He had a way with words, making my heart race with every sentence. I didn't know Axel for a long time, but from these brief text messages alone, I could tell he enjoyed nagging me. If he was standing in front of me, I'd probably hit him. He'd probably feed right off of that, too.

Don't you have a mountain to ski down???

You r right. I'll bug you later.

Please don't.

I don't believe you.

I hesitated, letting my thumb hover just above the touch screen.

Sure. Whatever. Bug me if you want to.

He sent a heart emoji and an eagle emoji before I pocketed my phone. I took a deep breath, taking myself down from this sneaky side flirting I had going on with Axel. As much as I was getting a high from doing it, it left me with a foul taste in my mouth. Axel was fun. Fresh. And the friends with benefits thing was still a thing.

It was fine.

I looked back toward Kala's RV. She and Pete were making their way to our site. She had a small pack strapped across her back. A good pair of hiking boots adorned her feet next to Pete's and her hair braided across her shoulder. She had on an orange t-shirt with each sleeve tied at her shoulders with hair ties and a pair of dark cargo shorts. I didn't realize how petite she was until seeing her bare arms and legs.

Pulling my kinky curls up into a bun, I smiled as they came to the car.

"Happy you came."

She shrugged. "Yeah. Well, it beats hanging out here with my dad moping around all day."

"And she has trail mix and astronaut ice cream." Pete closed his eyes and sighed at the sound of those two unrelated words.

I raised a brow. "Astronaut ice cream?"

"It's so good. Like a guilty pleasure." Pete smiled at Kala. "I haven't had any in so long."

"It's freeze-dried sugar." Kala turned her bag around and unzipped it, pulling out the space delicacy Pete was melting over. "See."

I shook my head. "That sounds . . . disgusting."

"It's not for everyone." She put it back in her bag.

Unclipping the keys from my short loop, I tossed them to Pete. "You're driving."

He lifted his arm, letting the key reflect in the sunlight. "Let the adventure begin!"

Kala held in a giggle, bringing her hands to her mouth. I rolled my eyes from behind my sunglasses and opened the car door. "Turn off the nerd for one day, please?"

"Never," Pete said as he climbed into the driver's seat and Kala was in the back. As soon as the doors closed, the car purred to life, rolling through the dirt and up toward the highway.

Pete sat back in the driver's seat with the sunshade down. Needing glasses prevented him from enjoying the relief of a pair of shades. His shaggy blond hair blew in the wind like raised hands on a super fast roller coaster. One elbow leaned against the open window as the other kept the wheel steady. I pulled up the strap on my tank top, leaning against the back of the chair. With a quick glance, I spied Kala gazing dreamily out of the back window, a pair of turquoise headphones wrapped around her ears.

She must have spotted me staring because she glanced at me, bringing her hands forward like I caught her doing something wrong. With a smirk, I tapped my studded ears against the arms of my sunglasses. "What are you listening to?"

Kala peeled off her headphones before returning her hands to her lap. "The 1975."

"Wanna put it on the radio?"

She lowered her chin, taking a quick glance at Pete before returning to me. "If that's okay with you."

"I wouldn't ask if it wasn't okay." I poked Pete in the arm, catching his attention. "Put up the windows a bit. Kala's got some tunes."

Hitting the door, the windows slid up halfway, cutting the sounds of the rushing air in half. "What's on the menu?"

"The 1975." I pressed the Bluetooth button on the dash. "You got Bluetooth on your phone, Kala?"

She nodded, attending to her phone to get it connected.

"Aren't The 1975 kinda poppy?" Pete asked.

"I don't like their poppy stuff too much," Kala responded. "But their older stuff is great."

"We're all about trying it." Pete smirked as the speakers announced the successful connection. "Well, everything. Except for country."

"I hate country music. But bluegrass is okay."

"Bluegrass?" My brows furrow. "Like Bob Dylan?"

"Mumford? Ever heard of them?"

"I have."

"They're pretty sweet," Pete said, glancing at me. "I doubt they're your cup of tea."

"Cup of tea?" I lower my shades. "Are you British now?"

"Less talking. More listening." He glanced back at Kala. "Press play and let's hear some '75."

With slight hesitation, she looked at her phone before her finger touched the screen. A low hum came up from the speakers as a youthful voice softly rose in the car. It only lasted a minute or two before pops of beats kept time with the lyrics. It was catchy. Definitely something I could dance to instantly. My fingers tapped against the seats as my body reacted to the music pumping through my ears. A subtle bob took over Pete's head as well. His eyes relaxed as we continued down the road. The song reached a point where the poppy notes scratched as the vocals grew harsher, with muddled words decorating the sound. It immediately grew again, back to the smooth synthetic sounds as the chorus carried it off into the ending notes.

"Shit." I smiled, looking at Kala. "That was awesome. What song was that?"

"'Somebody Else' I think it's called." Her voice carrying a bit more confidence now.

"That sounded a lot like Chvrches," Pete added

"Churches? That's not some Christian group, is it?" I asked.

"I have plenty of their songs on my phone, too." Kala didn't wait for permission this time as she scanned her phone once again, and another song erupted through the speakers.

"Nice!" Pete immediately grooved as the sound filled the car.

As soon as the sweet vocals grew from the music, he sang along with an almost nonexistent voice. Kala watched him with a sweet smirk, joining in as the two of them continued their impromptu car karaoke. Their singing grew louder as the chorus kicked in. I couldn't help but laugh, watching the passion Pete was putting into it. His excitement loosened the uncertainty in Kala's demeanor as she also raised the volume on her much better singing abilities.

They kept up their singing till the end, which I applauded with overly exaggerated clapping. "You two should start a band."

"Man, 'Lies' gets me pumped every time." Pete hadn't stopped smiling since the song kicked on. He looked back at Kala. "Your musical taste gets an 'A' in my book."

"I saw them in concert last year. Got to meet them and everything. They are super chill." Kala had fully removed herself from her shyness. It was kind of adorable to see how excited she was. Pete kept adding more logs on her fire with his shared enthusiasm. I felt the hairs on the back of my neck stand up again. Their conversation sounded muffled in my ears, and I could only focus on their faces. They were having fun talking about music that I couldn't add my two cents to. Kala leaned off the seat, holding onto the edge of Pete's chair. My focus was stuck there. How close her hand was to his shoulder. She wasn't trying anything. It was innocent. That's what I kept telling myself. It's just an innocent conversation.

"What did you think, Ash?"

My gaze shot to Pete. I opened my mouth, but no words came out. Pete raised his brow. "You okay?"

"Yeah. Totally okay." I adjusted myself in my seat to shake the unsettled feeling from my bones. "Definitely loved it. It was kind of sexy, in an aggressive sort of way."

"Yeah?" Kala twists her mouth. "I never would have thought that."

"Well, Ash has a one-track mind. If you know what I mean." My hand instinctively swatted across Pete's shoulder at that remark. He pulled back, a breath-filled chuckle escaping his permanent smirk. "I'm driving here!"

The incident spread a nervous smile across Kala's face. A stifled giggle rumbled behind her partially closed mouth. With a long sigh, I leaned against the headrest and rested my chin on my arm. "Anything goes."

Kala set her smile free as she leaned back against the bench. Letting her guard down didn't seem to come easy for her. But it made sense, being that she was living out of an RV with her drunk father. We all have our demons. They look different from everyone else's. I just hoped we could help her forget about hers for just a little while longer.

fourteen

. . .

south dakota, sunday, august 2nd

"SORRY, we sold the tour out for the day."

Pete and I looked at each other as we stood in the Wind Cave National Park Visitor Center. Wood-paneled walls hung behind black and white photos and weathered maps in sun-bleached frames. Stuffed bison decorated a few of the display tables. The ranger, wearing glasses and a uniform with a shiny badge, stood behind a big wooden desk with a tall, triple-layered display case.

"What else is there to do around here?" Pete asked the ranger.

"There's plenty of hiking trails. Tons of wildlife in the area, prairie dog town and bison trail. The natural entrance hike is probably the most popular. Also, there's camping up at Elk Mountain. First come first serve if you're looking for a few days in the wilderness." He pulled out a map and slid it across the table. "Everything you can see and do is right here."

"Thanks." Pete took the map and smiled. "Appreciate the information."

"Of course." The ranger smiled and tipped his head. "I'm here if you have questions."

The three of us left the desk and headed for the door. Pete already had the map open, pouring over the lines and markings showing trails, picnic areas, and the campground entrance.

Pete turned to me with a smile, and I couldn't help but return one. He smelled like sunblock and bubblegum. He chewed so much bubblegum; I bet it was a baseball thing. I'd tell him to stop if I didn't love it so much.

Reaching over him, I point to one of the trail markers on the map. "Let's do the natural entrance hike. Might be cool."

Kala came up on the right, glancing at the map with quiet hesitation. "It's the only natural entrance to the cave. Lakota legend says it was the passageway in which humans came to walk the earth."

"That's pretty cool." Pete glanced at her. "Did you learn that in school?"

"No." Kala shook her head. "My dad . . . I'm half Lakota."

"Be careful." I moved around Pete and came next to Kala. "Pete's gonna talk your ear off about it now that he knows."

Pete raised his brow above his frames as he lowered the map. "I will not." He glanced at Kala. "I mean . . . if it bothers you, I won't."

A quick shrug flushed Kala's cheeks with rosy embarrassment. "I . . . guess I don't mind."

We were still pretty lacking in our knowledge of who Kala was before meeting her at the campground. But from what I observed, she was unsure of herself. She lacked confidence in a multitude of areas, and pleasing people was something she was clearly used to doing. As much as it pained me to admit, I saw a lot of myself in her. The girl I had been after my dad died. Only Kala wasn't angry or impulsive. Not yet. Maybe that would change the deeper she fell into the pit that her father had banished her into.

Stepping out into the warm sun, I pulled my sunglasses back over my eyes, breathing in the dry summer air. The highway stretched out before us, leading cars in a single, solitary direction.

"We'll need to drive a bit to get to the trailhead. But it's not too far." Pete looked at me as I leaned against his shoulder, touching my nose with his. "Shall we?"

"Lead the way."

I didn't think I'd ever experienced air like this. Walking across the rolling hills and endless stretches of green was like something out of a Disney movie. I was having a complete *Beauty and the Beast* moment when Belle ran in the open field, belting out a song of hope. I would have taken my hair down if it wasn't a pain in the ass to manage. Standing on one of the rocky foothills, I closed my eyes and inhaled a long drag of the Dakota wind tearing through the treeless hills.

Someone stepped beside me, casting a shadow over my eyelids. Not being sure if it was Pete or Kala, I let myself lean against them, hoping it was who I wanted it to be. When an arm slid around my waist and pulled me close, I knew I'd assumed correctly. Pete planted a kiss on the side of my head as I opened my eyes with a smile.

"It's fucking gorgeous out here," I said as I nestled against his shoulder.

"I know. Nothing like New York, huh?"

"New York can kiss my ass."

We continued our vigil overlooking the plains. It was almost noon, and the sun was unblemished in the vast blue of the sky. I couldn't think of anything that would make this more perfect.

"We aren't too far from the entrance." Kala's voice turned both our heads. She was standing farther up the trail on the side of the ascending cliff. The map held tightly in her hand.

Pete nodded. "All right. Let's see this thing." Pete's arm dragged across my waist and found my hand, lacing his fingers in between mine as he led me up the trail.

The path wasn't challenging, but it was a bad idea to wear Converse. My feet were crying out in pain with every step. I tried not to show my struggle, but it wasn't improving. Especially when the trail went up at an almost 90-degree angle. Wedging my flat shoes into the rocks only stressed the radiating ache in my heels.

A slight vibration rattled against my leg. Text message. I pulled out my phone and flashed on the screen. Axel's face popped up as I tapped on the message.

AXEL

North Dakota is shaping up to be a huge bust.
What are you up to?

"You okay?" Pete looked at me questioningly, his eyebrow half raised.

Forcing a smirk, I pocketed my phone and looked down at my feet with a bit of regret. "I wore the wrong shoes for this." Luckily, the soreness I felt in my feet could easily push that text from my mind. "Why didn't you tell me to change my shoes?"

He shrugged. "I don't know. I didn't think about it." He looked me up and down, raising both eyebrows. "Want me to carry you?"

Twisting the corner of my mouth, I leaned to the right as my hand came across my hips. "You're serious?"

"Uh, yeah. Why wouldn't I be?"

"You're not gonna pull any funny business, are you?"

He scoffed, shaking his head at my sarcastic caution. "You think I'm gonna throw you off the cliff or something?" He came in front of me, taking off his backpack before looking over his shoulder. "Hop on."

With an exaggerated sigh, I took his backpack and strapped it on my back. "Okay." Bracing myself, I hopped up, wrapping my arms around his neck loosely. His hands immediately hooked around my legs, arms locking under my knees as I settled against him. "I'm not gonna fall, am I?"

"Don't worry." He hopped to shift me on his back once before adjusting his footing. "I got you."

He took a step forward, and a small part of me braced for the worst. But he remained steady, keeping me secure. My arms relaxed around his neck without losing my grip. I rested my chin on his shoulder, taking in the dwindling sunscreen scent of his skin. I couldn't stop myself from kissing him if I wanted to. Who said I wanted to?

"My big strong Andy."

"Yeah, totally pulling a Claire right now."

My head came off his shoulder. "Claire?"

"Yeah. You think Ally would be caught dead doing this?"

"Claire like . . . *Breakfast Club* Claire?" Kala asked.

I forgot Kala was walking in front of us. She kept her pace but glanced to catch our attention. Pete did a quick stop, his posture straightening with surprise. "Wow. Point for Kala. You're a *Breakfast Club* aficionado too?"

"I don't know about that. But I like the movie."

"I knew there was something special about you."

Kala's eyes shifted. "Liking the *Breakfast Club* makes me special?"

"It makes you something to us."

A nervous breath escaped her lips. "Okay." Kala whipped her head around to continue forward, quickening her pace.

"Something I said?" he asked quietly as we continued to follow her.

I leaned in next to his ear. "She's shy around you. Probably because you're so damn good looking."

"Oh, am I? I hadn't noticed."

"You know you are."

"Maybe I just like to hear you say it."

"Hmm." I tighten my hold around his neck, bringing my lips closer to his cheek, kissing the corner of his mouth. "I could say much, much dirtier things if you want me to."

"Wow. That is very un-Claire-like of you." He turned slightly to catch my lips.

I relished in his sweet summer taste. "Claire would totally do that. She's a tease, remember?"

"Yeah, you're one hundred percent a tease." He turned and pecked the side of my face. "Behave yourself. We can't leave Kala alone."

A breathy huff left me deflated on his shoulder. "I'll be good."

Staring down at this hole in the rock was far less entertaining than I originally hoped. It was small. Maybe big enough for a child to fit through, and that was it. There was a flat grassy square just outside of it and a shrewdly made set of craggy stairs leading down to it. I folded my arms, trying to imagine what kind of story went along with this historical place.

"This was a pathway to the spirit lodge."

We both looked at Kala as she stared down at the hole. But it wasn't just a hole to her as her words led me to believe.

"What is the spirit lodge?" Pete asked.

Kala bent to rest on her knees. "It's the place humans waited for the Earth to be prepared for them." She pointed to the entrance. "This is *Oniya Oshoka*, the passageway to Earth. The Wind Cave is where the Earth draws breath. A portal to the spirit lodge lies inside. According to the stories."

"Wow, that's pretty cool." Pete walked next to Kala as she drew to a stand. She glanced at him with a weak smile before looking back down at the entrance to the cave.

"They came through that small hole?" I asked, pointing to the entrance again.

"The Creator shrank it so no human could pass through it again. Left as a reminder of where they came from."

Pete put his hands in the pockets of his shorts, glancing back at me momentarily. "Is your name Native American too?"

"Yeah." Kala hesitated, pressing her lips together before letting out a nervous breath. "Zitkala means little bird."

"Cool." He took a step back. "You should be proud of your heritage. It's important not to lose it."

Kala shrugged, keeping her eyes fixed on the entrance of the mountain. "It feels like a burden sometimes." Her eyes widened as she came round to see if we had heard what she said. "Sorry. I—"

"What is there to be sorry for?" I hopped around them, grabbing Kala's arm. "I get it. I know what it's like living in the shadows of the past."

Kala looked at me, her eyes settling. "Something my dad refuses to let me forget, unfortunately." Glancing back at Pete, another tempered smile raised her high cheekbones. "But I am proud. Sometimes. Depending on the day."

Pete smiled as he looked up into the endless sky. "Sometimes I wish I was something cooler. Like . . . Norwegian or something."

I pressed my eyebrows down above my eyes. "Norwegian? Don't you have half of Europe's blood in your veins?"

Pete shrugged. "I don't know. Irish. Yes. And a hundred other things."

A low bellow echoed up from the rolling plains below. Kala's head turned, holding onto my wrist as she inched toward the opposite side of the cliff. "Come on."

My feet moved behind her, climbing another 100 feet up before reaching the edge. Kala stopped and watched with patient eyes. As I followed her gaze, I had to catch my breath at the spotted scene below. There must have been fifty to sixty bison scattered across the pale green hills. I'd seen these things on nature shows all the time, but holy shit. Standing above them, even though we weren't right next to them, their presence was jaw dropping. Big, majestic animals with tall shoulders and heads as big as a Volkswagen Bug.

"Woah." I didn't blink as we stood there, watching them eat their weight in the grass. A few grunts and deep calls rolled up and played through the acoustics that the landscape had provided.

Pete came up beside me, a long drawn out breath flowing from his lips. "Holy . . . "

I looked at Kala. Her face was beaming, like this was her own personal little herd of brown beasts. I pulled her closer to me, returning with a smile of my own as we all stood in silence at what lay before us.

The roadside diner could not be any more perfect. We sat in a booth, my elbow leaning against the window as I stared at the waning sun in the distance. The seats had a red and white plastic awning, and the table was that classic yellow sponge color with shiny aluminum siding. The bar stretched across half the length of the entire one-floor building. There were a few other people dotting the stools, letting aproned waitresses fill their cups with coffee.

Pete pulled his arm off the booth seat. "Order me a cherry coke. I gotta hit the bathroom."

I turned and nodded assuringly as he slipped off the seat. He followed the bar until it curved to the left before disappearing beyond the diner window. My phone went off in my pocket and I quickly remembered Axel's text from before. I slipped it out of my pocket and checked the screen.

AXEL

Did you fall off a cliff or something?

Biting my lower lip, I sat criss-cross in the seat as I searched for a picture I took of Kala, Pete, and me overlooking the bison roaming the plains below us. With a simple tap, I attached it to the message.

ASHLEY

Epic hike at the Wind Cave. Pretty sweet day.

Nice. Who's the other girl?

Someone we met. She's been hanging with us.

You make friends wherever you go.

You think I'm your friend? You misjudged that one.

I'm somethin, aren't I?

A subtle smirk flashed across my face. I let my finger linger there, not sure what I should say in reply. But he beat me to it.

When am I gonna c you again, anyway?

He wanted to see me again. Shit. I'd be lying if I said I said I didn't want to. Because I wanted to. He had been fun to mess with during our last encounter. And all this texting back and forth was soon becoming a treat to partake in. Maybe I should see him again. Or maybe I should just drop it and focus on the perfect guy right in front of me.

It was becoming increasingly difficult not to act on my impulses. To put on the old Ashley mask and live a little dangerously again. It wasn't wrong.

No strings, right?

"Pete's a nice guy."

I dropped my phone facedown on the table and looked at Kala. She was watching me, her hands folded in front of her on the table. "What?"

"Pete. He's such a nice guy." She looked down at her hands for a second. "You two are perfect together."

"Oh." Shaking what felt like spiderwebs from my face, I flashed an uneasy smile. "We aren't together."

Kala's eyes flashed unexpectedly. "Oh . . . I thought you . . . "

"Back." Pete swung around the booth and slid next to me.

Kala's eyes darted from me to him, and back again. All I could do was stare at her. Something felt wrong about admitting that we weren't together. Saying it out loud made my back tense and my legs buckle.

"So, what are we ordering?" Pete unfolded the menu with eager anticipation. "I say we order a pile of junk."

Pete's love of food loosened the tension around the subject, letting me fall comfortably back into my skin. "You are such a pig."

"Why not?" He looked up at Kala. "Unless you're against greasy diner food?"

She shook her head. "No, I like onion rings and fries as much as the next person."

"Nice. I think we have a unanimous decision." He gave me that adorable raised eyebrow look. "What do you say, Claire?"

Damn. I had a hard time with that face. It was like he was tempting me to cross the line every time. And maybe he was. In a perfect Pete world, we'd be peas and carrots, mac and cheese, ice cream, and a cherry. But my life was far from perfect, so why should my relationships be any different?

With a tight fist, I threw down the menu, pinning it to the table with a fist. "If I say yes, will you stop calling me Claire?"

"If you say yes, you totally don't deserve to be called Claire."

But I was Claire. And that's what made it so hard. I was a tease. A total bitch. A full-of-myself snob with a poor attitude and a broken life. I had to prove to myself that I could change. It was the only way I could finally make sense of all this garbage I was trying to sift through.

Axel. I had to make it happen. Even if Pete never understood why.

fifteen

. . .

BACK AT THE CAMPSITE, Kala and I sat by the small fire pit in the cool South Dakota night. We spent the day hanging around, taking some much needed time for our muscles and feet to rest after yesterday's hike. Pete let Kala read some of his comic books, which her nose was in for most of the day. He got on his board and could quench his skater boy bug for a bit. Overall, it was a simple day. Though I still haven't responded to Axel's request for when he'd see me again.

The sky was littered with stars. You could barely see the darkness behind it. I had a fuzzy blanket wrapped around me on the bench. Kala was on the opposite side, sitting cross-legged with her arms around her waist. Pete was on the phone with his bestie, Logan.

Axel's last text ate at me, trying to figure out how to make things happen without actually making them happen. That made little sense, even to me. I wasn't sure what I could say that wouldn't make me sound desperate. This usually came naturally to me, but now that I was actively trying to bring us back together, it became a chore.

"Can I ask you something?" Kala glanced at me, her face turned downward, letting her long hair fall into her face.

I focused on her, stuffing my thoughts into the corner of my skull. "Shoot."

She adjusted herself to sit a little straighter before wandering to the flickering flames. "If you and Pete aren't a couple, what are you?"

I didn't realize how confusing this situation might seem to others. Frankly, I didn't care. The thought of responding to that question made me realize how I was disregarding our relationship. "Friends with benefits, but I don't know. To be honest," I said with a sigh. The next words pinned to the back of my throat. I had to shake it free with a forced cough or I'd choke on them and never get them out. "I was in a real shitty relationship before we came on this trip. I was stuck and didn't want to get out of it."

"Why didn't you want to?" Kala squinted as she looked at me. I could only shrug and drop my shoulders like a load of bricks.

"It was comfortable. And complicated. I didn't think I deserved better." A huff of mild exhilaration escaped me. "But, Pete. He stepped in one night. Totally unannounced. Told my boyfriend to back off and leave me alone. I didn't know who he was or why he did it." My gaze wandered to the fire. "I got the bug, you know? I wanted to know everything about him after that. What he liked, what his life was like. It drove me crazy. We hung out a few times, and I felt like I could relax around him. Be myself. I loved it. But I had to end it with the asshole. And I did. Pete gave me space. And after it was done, I thought I was ready to be with him."

I looked down at the horizontal pattern of the blanket, watching the firelight pulse against it in the night. "But I'm petrified. I feel like a little kid. Like my dad died all over again, and I had no one. I wasn't worth shit to anybody. Not even to myself."

"Wait. Your dad died?"

My head shot up to Kala, whose eyes were wide with concern. I said too much. The hair on the back of my neck stood erect. The beating of my heart was so intense, my ribs were in danger of cracking. Shooting to my feet, I stared vacantly out into the empty night, my feet commanding me to get the hell out of there. "I . . . need a minute."

Turning toward the camper, I hustled without looking back, even when I heard Kala call my name. The unwanted emotions welled up inside of me. I hated crying. I would not cry. My emotions didn't matter. Never had I allowed myself to be so open and vulnerable with someone I barely knew.

That was Pete rubbing off on me. It was a mistake. This whole thing was a mistake.

Rushing behind the camper, I rested my head against its smooth surface. Deep, labored breaths tried to quell the rising tide of my vulnerability with little effect. Closing my eyes, I tried to count to myself. Random shit like that would work sometimes. But as the darkness of my eyelids enveloped my vision, all I could think about was sitting in the hospital room after my dad had died. My mom running from the room, leaving me alone with tears in my eyes as I stared at the shell of my father.

"Hey." My eyes shot open, turning toward Pete's slow encroachment. "You okay?"

I wanted to run and shed my tears all over him. To smell his comforting scent and feel his arms around me. But my mind was playing tricks on me again, and all I could think of was how he made me feel things I was afraid to feel. How he made me pliable. I was okay with not caring. Okay with forgetting. But he brought everything back.

"No. No, I'm not okay, Pete." The longer I looked at him, the faster my pulse raced. My walls were up and the archers were ready to defend it. "This." I pointed to him and me. "I'm not okay with this."

Taken aback, his posture shifted into awareness. "What are you talking about?"

"Nothing, just . . . " I turned away from him with the lies conjuring inside of me. "I need some space, okay?"

"Fine."

I listened his sneakers shuffle through the dusty ground and away from my ears. Hot tears continued to plague my eyes, but I refused to let them fall. I couldn't get inside the camper fast enough. When I closed the door and locked it behind me, I crashed onto the bed, letting the flood gates open with no resistance.

I don't think I could have shut my eyes any tighter. The moment I cast my sight into darkness, my dad was there, in his casual baggy shirt and cargo shorts. Waves cascading down to his shoulders in a sea of glossy blond. That smile my mom swore I stole straight from his face, framing his perfect white teeth. And his eyes were as blue as the Midwest sky.

"Dad," I whispered. "Tell me what to do. Please . . . tell me what to do."

I wish he could make everything stop. If only to give me a chance to breathe. He always knew how to calm me down. Whether it was crying over a dropped ice cream cone or recovering from brotherly teasing.

"Take a second, ladybug," he'd say with his thick Australian accent. His hands would always brace my shoulders, bending down so he was constantly level with my eyes. "Breathe in. Breathe out."

He called me ladybug. How could I forget something like that?

I tried to abide, but I couldn't stop myself from succumbing to copious amounts of tears. So, I just let it be, thinking on his words as I never have before and wishing like crazy he was there to help me figure out this mess I had created for myself.

sixteen

. . .

south dakota, monday, august 3rd

I DIDN'T KNOW how long I was lying there. My eyes were puffy and throbbing from all the unbridled disappointment that fell from them. I reached up to the shelf before my fingers wrapped around the keepsake box I had stowed there before we left New York. Pulling it down, I opened the latch and drew the lid up. There was no fear behind my actions this time, only a stale numbness that I hadn't felt since I decided I didn't give a fuck about my life anymore.

There was a folded up piece of looseleaf paper the same length and width of the box. On top of it was a black-and-white photo of me and my dad from a photo booth, our tongues sticking out as we leaned playfully toward the camera. I couldn't stop a grin from splashing across my face as I looked at it, trying to dig up the memory from where I had buried it.

But I didn't have to.

I reached into the box, drawing the woven multicolored bracelet into my hands. Loose string hung from the adjustable chord that tied everything together. Without even stopping to contemplate, I passed my hand through it. The weight of it plummeted me into the sea of all the emotions I was trying to pull myself out of. It hit me like a brick to the chest and I practically heaved as I pulled it taught against my skin.

It was heavy, so heavy I didn't think I could stand. But it felt familiar, like home.

My eyes followed every strand of color as it wove into the pattern. Where the threads crossed was a mix of dark and light shades, like the chaos of an unbalanced life trying to readjust itself. But as soon as the strands met, it unfolded, becoming a singular hue before clashing all over again.

I never realized how much this bracelet was me, the pattern of my actions and my choices. The footprints I had left behind.

There was a knock on the door. I shut the box and placed it back on the shelf as a gentle voice came from the outside. "Ash. It's Kala."

Slowly, I crawled along the bed and reached for the handle, opening the door to let her in. Kala climbed in, sat on the bed, and took her shoes off before coming next to me with her heels folded neatly under her. She watched me, her eyes darting in all directions as she witnessed how pathetic I was.

How could I ever apologize for what I'd said to Pete?

"Are you okay?"

Despite my efforts, I couldn't muster even the slightest grin. "I guess. I don't know."

She licked her lips nervously. "I'm really sorry. About your dad."

"Yeah." My eyes fell to Gremlin, who was rubbing against my arm. "I am too." I raised my hand to scratch behind his ears, which he graciously accepted. Kala waited in the silence with me, listening to the gentle purrs of a satisfied cat as he basked in attention. It was easier with him. Cats make everything bearable, even if it's only for a little while.

"Was he a good dad?"

Kala's question got me thinking. I didn't know the full extent of how shitty her dad had been, but her question seemed more like one of awe at the fact that yes, there were good dads out there. But good wasn't a big enough word to describe my dad to anyone. "He was. My everything." My hand came back down on Gremlin's soft face, who had not abandoned his purring onslaught.

"Sometimes I think it would be better if my dad died." Kala's head was down, nervously playing with her fingers in her lap. "I failed him. He'd be better off dead." A few loose tears fall into her palms.

I reached for her, grabbing her by the shoulders. "Don't say that." I brushed the trail of tears coating her cheeks. "How your dad acts is not your fault."

Her lower lip quivered as she opened her mouth to speak. "But I could have . . . been a better daughter."

"Kala." I nudged her, making sure she was looking at me dead in the eyes. Any sense of feeling sorry for myself was gone at this point. This girl was as lost and broken as I was. Only she had hope. She wasn't too far gone, or at least I had to believe that she wasn't.

"If he can't change for you, he never will. That's on him. Not you. Okay?"

"Okay." Her response was so weak, I didn't believe she heard me.

"You're amazing. If he can't see how amazing you are and won't fight to keep you, he's the asshole. He failed you."

Kala lost all control of herself, melting into my shoulder to let the waterfall of her sadness wash over me. I held on to her, wrapping my arms around her small frame like my life depended on it. I could feel the dam well up behind my eyes, but I held on because I had to be strong for her. For once in my life, I had to be strong for someone other than myself.

"I know it's hard . . . to see that. Sometimes you don't want to see it. But you can't keep blaming yourself for what he is." The words shocked me into revelation. I was trying to comfort her, but I was realizing these were words I neglected to live by for a long time.

I could have never fixed Wes. Never. He didn't want my help, only someone to throw all his shit onto. That was all I was. A scapegoat. A way for him to get heat off himself and not feel bad that he didn't have the gall to fight his own battles. And I let him. I let myself believe I was making it better. The sad thing was, I didn't know any better. Not until Pete showed me what someone would do for someone else.

"Okay." Kala didn't leave, and I held her for what felt like hours. I didn't care. I'd be there until she was all cried out. Maybe I could make her realize she had to get out before she was too far gone. Before she ended up like me.

seventeen

. . .

south dakota, tuesday, august 4th

THE MORNING CARRIED an uneasy haze throughout the campground. I sat staring at the last traces of smoke trailing upward toward the waning morning sky. My red Beats headphones pumping some much needed Joy Division to distract me from myself. A yawn escaped me as I let my left foot sway just above the ground. I wrapped Kim's jacket around me to keep the chilly morning at bay. But the coldness of the day was piercing through my skin, but I wondered if it was also seeping into my soul.

I looked over toward Kala's RV. Her dad was outside smoking a cigarette. The surrounding air had shrouded his face in a hazy gray. He must have noticed me staring, because he looked at me with tired eyes. I watched him, wishing I had the will to go over there and tell him what an asshole he was. But I felt completely defeated after last night.

After Kala had left, I fell into a deep, troubling sleep, plagued by dreams of Wes' ugly mug cursing me out as I reached for him to pull me from the ocean I was drowning in.

The knife in my heart hurt more when I realized Pete wasn't there when I woke up.

My phone buzzed, and I looked down, seeing a heart and hug emoji sent from Kala. I smiled, sending her one straight back. After I swiped to my messages on the screen, I saw Axel toward the top, his question still lingering in the unanswered section of my mind. I didn't have the energy to answer him now, or maybe ever.

The air felt heavy as I directed my attention to the ground. I could feel Pete's presence like a falcon circling its prey. He likely didn't mean it to come off that way, but my emotional state made me an easy target for interrogation.

"Wanna take a walk with me?" he asked in a low tone.

Shifting my eyes, I could finally see his brows slightly creased with uncertainty as he pushed his glasses up the bridge of his nose. A feeling of dread twisted in my gut, but I couldn't avoid dealing with this any longer.

"Sure."

The hills that rolled around the campground we had called home for the past week looked endless, despite the conditions of the day. Pete and I trekked across the trail leading away from the camp, mostly in silence. My water bottle clung to my denim knapsack, slightly gracing the bare skin exposed from my shorts. I tied a bandana across my forehead to keep my curly locks out of my face.

Pete wore a Yankees cap to avoid the bright sun that was made worse by the cloudy sky. He walked in front of me with his own bag and water bottle, eyes to the landscape and nowhere else. Usually I wasn't afraid to get right into it, but today was different. Words kept getting stuck in my mouth like flies in honey. I felt kinda queasy, and ignoring it didn't help. I knew I had to clear the air, no matter how hard it would be. But lighting the match was nearing impossible levels.

We walked along a hilltop toward the down slope, before coming up again. Even though my feet were as heavy as bricks, I scurried up beside Pete, catching his attention for a split second.

"Hey," was about the only thing I could think to say.

He didn't respond right away, just continued walking for a minute, looking ahead. "Hey."

I walked around a jutting rock before coming back beside him. "I'm sorry I said those things to you. I didn't mean it."

"No, you did," he said, so matter-of-factly it cut through me like a harsh winter chill.

I was walking on eggshells and, for the first time, I was the one trying to be careful not to break too many. Pete was willingly stomping all over them. His entire demeanor deflated.

"Look." He stopped to face me. When his eyes met mine, they softened, like I made him weak. But he quickly recovered, returning to a state of determination and grit. "We can't keep doing this. One day you're jumping all over me, talking dirty in my ear, and the next, you're running at me with your mouth on fire, ready to burn me. I . . . " He huffed. "What kind of person do you think I am?"

I shrugged, letting the question hang with my mouth agape, unable to think of anything to say that would satisfy him. "I don't know what you wanna hear."

"The truth would be nice."

"I can't give you the truth." I looked away into the tormented sky. "It changes every day."

"Changes how?" I returned to his eagerness for answers. "About me?"

"Pete—"

"I've been nothing but honest with you. Why can't you grant me the same courtesy?"

"That's not who I am." He took a few steps away, his hands resting on the top of his cap. "Don't you already know that?"

I let him be alone with his thoughts for a minute, wishing he would just walk away entirely and leave me there like anyone else would. But he didn't. He stood with his back to me. I waited like a kid about to be scolded, feeling the emotional rise clutch at my chest with each breath.

Pete's hands came down at his sides. With a slow turn, he took a step closer, watching me like he was waiting for someone to take off my head. "Look, your flaws are part of who you are. They don't scare me. I've told you that."

"Maybe they scare me, okay?" I had to bite my tongue to keep myself from falling apart. "Maybe I don't trust myself to do the right thing. Or I don't want to do the right thing. I don't know."

"What is the right thing for you?"

I dropped my head toward the ground as a subtle breeze rustled the sand-coated grass at our feet. "I . . . I don't know."

In what felt like a split second, Pete's scuffed-up Airwalks came into view across from my purple Converse. I looked up as he took my arms in his hands. He was firm, but only for a minute before his grip softened.

"Ash, I . . . care about you a lot. Flaws and all. I know what I want. What's right for me. Figure out what you want without worrying about what I want. Until you do, we can't keep yo-yoing back and forth like this. It's not who *I* am."

"You're right." I didn't know if it was my sudden weakness to his touch or maybe I didn't feel worthy enough to have his hands on me, but I pulled away from him. "Are we gonna be okay?"

He sighed. "I don't know. I hope so."

"I want us to be okay." A few tears that had been stuck to the bottom of my well seeped from the corners of my eyes. "I care. I'm just . . . I'm trying."

"I know." Pete clasped his hands together, unsure of what to do with them. "I know you are, Ash. It's gonna be okay."

"No." I shook my head, looking out into the outstretched world beyond. "It's not."

eighteen

. . .

south dakota, friday, august 7th

IT WAS quiet the last few days we had stayed in the wagon circle. I spent a lot of time just chilling on the roof of the car with my headphones on, staring at the clear sky as the dry day sucked the moisture from my skin. Sometimes Gremlin laid on my chest, the natural warmth of him bringing some calm into my chaotic mind. Pete left me alone mostly, making small talk here and there.

It was awkward, the first night going to bed after our talk, keeping each other at arm's length. We both ended up falling asleep with the other in our gaze. He brushed the hair from my face and asked me how I was. I couldn't let go of his hand. I kept it close to me and he never pulled away. As much as I knew I needed to figure stuff out on my own, I was glad I wasn't alone.

Kala came by with hiking boots, khaki shorts, and a graphic tank that showed off her petite curves. She had her dark hair in pigtails which were hanging over her backpack straps. "Hey." She smiled. "Wanna take a hike?"

Pete sprang from his camping chair, throwing the comic he was reading into the seat. "Yeah. Sure. I'm down for a hike." He made his way to the camper. "Let me grab some stuff first."

He disappeared inside the camper. I sat up from my silent vigil of lounging across the picnic table with my headphones on. Immortal Girlfriend was pulsing in my ears, filling my mind with dreary dreams splattering across the canvas of my life. It didn't even look close to what Bob Ross could pull off in a half hour.

Kala turned and walked up to the table. "You coming too?"

I slipped one of my ears free from my headphones and turned to her. "I don't think I'm up for it."

"Oh, sure." Kala glanced back at the camper before coming back at me. "You okay?"

I slipped my sunglasses up to my forehead and squinted at her. "Fun fact about me. I'm never okay."

She tightened her lip and looked down at her feet. "I salute the light within your eyes where the whole universe dwells."

What she said sunk deep within the walls I'd built around myself as her eyes met mine. I sat up, sitting criss-crossed on the table. "What was that?"

She let out a nervous breath. "Nothing. Just a Lakota thing. I thought . . . " she swallowed, squeezing the straps of her bag across her shoulders. "It just felt appropriate. It's stupid."

"It's not stupid." I tried to swallow the quiet serenity those words planted in my throat. "What does it mean?"

She shrugged. "Whatever you think it means, I guess."

"Ready to go?" Pete hopped in beside her, drawing Kala's gaze. He had his backpack, hiking boots, and a water bottle hooked on the handle of his bag. His Yankee's hat kept his growing blond locks tucked safely back. He looked at me, his enthusiasm sagging into disappointment. "You coming?"

I shook my head as I managed another swallow to hide the impact of what Kala had said. "No. You two have fun. Don't get lost."

"Okay. Sure." Pete skidded across the dirt in front of Kala and set off.

Kala gave me a weak smile. "See you later, Ash."

I watched them head off together. They walked next to each other, Kala's hands still clutching her shoulder straps. I could hear them chatting, Pete doing most of the talking.

I salute the light within your eyes where the whole universe dwells.

My body came back down to the surface of the table, replacing my sunglasses over my eyes. How could I be proud of the light living inside a body plagued with corruption? The lack of definition gave the impression of a dream-like state, as if everything was slightly out of focus. I needed to get my shit together. My actions had consequences. And if I wanted to get over this hump of self-sabotage, I needed to act like I cared about how I affected the people around me. To cleanse the light so I could feel whole again.

My phone went off beside me. I grabbed it and lazily pressed accept without even bothering to see who it was as I brought it next to my ear.

"Yo." Dimitri's voice was both a welcomed relief, and a dreaded significance. "You've been standin' me up. What gives?"

I hadn't called him since we got here. With everything that's been happening, it completely slipped my mind. "Sorry." I sighed. "I've been distracted."

"Distracted? Did something happen?"

I bit my bottom lip. A lot of shit happened. Sex with Pete, nursing the wounds of a lost high schooler, juggling the idea of Axel, and my own chaotic determination to keep Pete at a distance. "Not really."

A frustrated sigh flooded my ears. "Don't pull this shit with me, Ash."

"What shit?"

"The same shit you pulled when Steve died. Telling me nothing was wrong all the damn time."

I shook my head, trying to relieve my mind of my dad's name. Nobody said his name since it happened and I didn't wanna know what it would do to me once it sank in. "That has nothing to do with this."

"You think I didn't notice you sneaking out every damn night? Comin' home and passing out in your room? I used to come in and clean you up, so Mom didn't see you all strung out and bruised when she got home after a three day shift."

My brow folded above my eyelids. "You did not."

"Don't tell me I didn't!" The authority in his voice widened my eyes beneath my sunglasses. "I couldn't say anything to you without you snappin' back. And Mom was too depressed to notice."

I tried to rake through my memories for any ounce of truth to his words. But there was nothing. I had woken up in different clothes, sometimes even tucked in to bed. But I never cared to think why, because I hated remembering back then. About how much I drank or who I might have slept with. If they forced me to do things or not, I had no clue. No evidence of anything. I wanted more, even if it meant ignoring the rubble of my life.

"Ash. *Ash!*"

Reality set in, and I sat up. "What?"

"Don't shut me out. You don't want to tell Mom, fine. You want to keep pulling shit, that's fine too. But please, don't shut me out. Don't keep me behind bars only to watch you fall again." A slow sigh gave him pause for a minute. "I hated leaving you with Mom after Steve died. But I couldn't stay. Because it was too hard to see you do that to yourself and not let me help you. And now. Now you seem different. Better. You're crawling out of it. Don't crawl back in. Please."

My chin shuttered as a few unexpected tears trickled from my eyes. I couldn't believe he cared so much back then. Maybe he had done everything he had said he did, or maybe he hadn't. None of that mattered. Because I could listen now and I heard him. Regret dripped from every word.

"Okay," I muttered, nodding like he could see me. "I'll try."

"You're stubborn as hell, but you're my sister. That ain't gonna change. Okay? I'll always be ready to listen. Whenever you're ready to talk."

"Okay." I sniffed, taking in a deep breath to settle my rattling nerves. "I hated when you left, you know? But I hated Ty even more."

"Damn, that piece of shit." Dimitri scoffed at the mention of our shunned sibling's name. "He's so full of himself. Guess he got it from somewhere."

"Probably your dad." I smiled as he laughed.

"Yeah, he definitely got it from that asshole." We shared a moment of relief from the scars of this conversation. When he settled, I could sense what words were coming next. "You don't got to tell me now if you don't want to. But don't hold it in, okay? Call me when you want to talk."

"Yeah, I will."

"Love you, Sis."

"Yeah." I sucked in a breath. "Love you too, D."

The sun was waning as it surrendered to the night. We were leaving for Mount Rushmore. It was a bit of a drive. We already attached the camper to the car, and we were just getting the last few things together before we left. Carrying Gremlin to the back seat, his carrier sat open for him to cross the bench next to Pete's skateboard.

He purred in my arms as his eyes squinted at the damaging South Dakota sun. Red headphones rested in front of my messy bun as I took one weary step at a time toward the car.

The lyrics of Radiohead's "Creep" crawled out of my mouth as it pulsed into my eardrums. I bent down to get Gremlin into the car.

He slipped into his carrier and I zipped it closed. Gremlin gave a satisfied meow before curling his body into a comfy warm circle. I came to a stand, staring at the light layer of earth coating the car. "I don't belong here . . . "

Movement on the other side of the car caught my eye. I didn't realize Pete was standing there, watching me with a veil of uncertainty flashing behind his dark-rimmed glasses. We watched each other. A weak twitch of my bottom lip stifled any sort of joy from being seen. I wanted to ask him what was wrong, but thought it was dumb. I already knew what was wrong.

Pulling my headphones off, they landed around my neck. "We ready to go?"

Kala said she would come to say her goodbyes before we left, but she was nowhere in sight. I couldn't tell if Pete was disappointed because of that or still hanging on the edge of the cliff that was our relationship.

A slight nod drew the corners of his mouth up into a half grin. It was infectious, and I flashed a quick smile of my own. "Want me to drive?"

"No, I'll—" Something caught his eye as he shifted to my left. Squinting, I turned around to catch what it might be. "Shit."

Kala was running across the circle toward us, her dad screaming and shouting as he, too, dropped out of the RV door. She had a bag with her and blankets and clothes wrapped in her arms. I pulled away from the car as she got closer, Pete coming around to meet me on the other side. The closer she came, the more I could see how distressed her face was.

My feet moved as fast as hers, closing the gap between us. Pete wasn't too far behind. When she reached the edge of our site, she fell on one knee, breathless sobs escaping her mouth. "I can't anymore. I can't be there . . . "

"Whoa, calm down." I put my hands on her shoulders and helped her up. In the distance, her dad was back on his feet, stumbling across the circle in drunken belligerence.

"I called my mom," Kala breathed. "I need to get to California." Her brown soaked eyes looked from me to Pete. "Please. Can you take me with you? She's said it's okay. I just . . . I can't be here another second. Please."

I shot Pete a look, who seemed immediately against the idea. Kala was a minor at seventeen.

"Kala—" Pete started, but I cut him off quickly.

"Get in the car."

"Really?" Her eyes brightened at my immediate response.

"Ash, we could get in serious trouble."

I turned to Pete. "We can't leave her here." Wrapping my arm around her shoulders, I rushed Kala to the back seat of the car. "Get in and buckle up."

She didn't protest, climbing into the seat and shutting the door behind her. Pete walked to the driver's side as I opened the door. "I'll drive."

I didn't argue and jumped over the hood to ride shotgun. We both got in as Kala's father breached the circle. "*Zitkala!*" he screamed. "Get back here now!"

"Floor it!" I shouted as Pete turned the key and brought the car to life. I whipped out my phone from my pocket and got the camera on, recording everything that was about to happen.

Hands crashed against the passenger side window. Kala fell back onto the seat. "Get away! I never want to see you again!"

"You're *not* going to your mom's! Kala. *Kala.* Get the hell out here!"

"Shit. Shit. Shit!" Pete slammed on the gas pedal as dust shot up from the tires, leaving a trail of smoke behind us. Kala's father ran after us, screaming, as we drove away with the camper. The car hit the bumps hard as we came to the exit. I held on to the back of the seat, watching Kala's father fade in the distance, coated by the dust we left behind.

"Get your seatbelt on!" Pete shouted at me as we crested the hill, hitting the ground hard. My head barely avoided crashing into the roof, so I turned around and threw the belt across my lap, clicking it securely to the seat.

We merged onto the highway, Pete cutting the wheel so tight, the force dragged me to the left. "Slow down!" I shouted. "We're clear!"

Glancing at Pete, his hands glued to the steering wheel with eyes wide. After a few labored breaths, he leaned back in the seat. His cheeks expanded as he blew air from his lungs.

"Fucking Batman level driving, Pete." I grabbed his arm, smiling so hard it hurt.

He glanced at me with a breathless sigh, shaking himself off before re-focusing on the road. "That was a rush." His eyes shifted to the rearview mirror. "You okay, Kala?"

I turned in my seat as Kala pulled the hair from her face. Her eyes were round and puffy from crying, but the adrenaline rush from our escape shut off the waterworks.

"Yeah. I think so."

I focused my phone on her, still recording. "Call your mom. Let her know you're on your way. Put her on speaker so we can talk to her, too." She wasn't able to focus as the emotion welled up behind her eyes again. I dropped my phone in my lap and reached for her hand, grabbing it tightly.

"Hey. Kala," tears rolled down her face as I captured her gaze, "it's gonna be okay."

Sniffing to subdue a few tears, she nodded with a weak smile. "You guys . . . I . . . " Kala took a deep breath. "Thanks."

nineteen

. . .

south dakota, saturday, august 8th

IT WAS CRAZY HOW FOUR PRESIDENTS' faces carved out of stone could draw such a crowd. Honestly, I think you could have carved any man's face into a mountain and people would flock to it. It was like I was being inaugurated myself as we walked toward Mount Rushmore. Flags flanked us on either side, swaying in the breeze of the mid-morning sun.

"Isn't this weird?" Pete eyed Kala as we walked past the few hundred waving flags. "I mean, most of these guys weren't that great."

"Lincoln ended slavery. And Washington . . . was kinda nice?" Kala shrugged. "The rest, I guess, were assholes."

"He was a wrestler, you know. Lincoln."

"A wrestler?" I raised a brow. "Like Andy?"

"Well, yeah, but it would be cool if he was like Macho Man." He raised his arms. "*Oh, yeah!*"

Kala smirked and raised her fingers to her mouth, like she was holding something small between her fingers. "Cream of the crop, oh yeah!"

"Oh! Score for Kala!" Pete raised his chin at me. "You could learn something from this."

"Wait, was Macho Man the pro-wrestler who wore yellow and red?"

"Wow." Pete's face dropped with an inescapable smirk. "I don't even have the energy to tell you how wrong you are."

"Whatever." I folded my arms. My phone buzzed in my messenger bag. Swinging it in front of me, I grabbed it out and saw it was Amber. "Amber's calling." I swiped to accept the call, and her sunglasses popped up on the screen. "Hey, girl."

"Hi, Amber!" Pete leaned in toward me and pushed his face right in front of me. "What's up?"

"Peter . . . you look well."

"How formal of you." He drew back and found my unamused face. "What?"

"Where are you guys now?" Amber asked. "There are a lot of flags . . . "

"Mount Rushmore." I pushed the camera button to flip the view, showing her the presidential skyline. "We're being watched by dead people."

"Fun. Who's the girl with you?"

Kala pushed her hair back, not wanting to get involved. I flipped the camera back around and stood next to her. "This is Kala. We're taking her to California to see her mom."

"What are you, a taxi service now?"

"We're picking up a masked hitch-hiker next." Pete pointed toward the phone. "Stay tuned."

I pulled the phone against my chest. "All right. Get out of here. Let me talk to Amber."

"Fine, have your girl talk. We'll be observing presidents." Pete nudged Kala's shoulder. "Stick with me."

"Oh. Okay." Kala glanced at me. "I can wait if you—"

"I'll catch up." I looked to at Pete. "Behave."

"You're telling *me* to behave?" Pete's eyes widened before letting out a stifled breath. "Sure. Whatever you say."

With a few steps back, I watched as they continued toward the mountain. Pete had his hands in his pockets, looking down at his feet. I pissed him off with my smart mouth. Again.

Every few steps, Kala got closer and closer to him, without actually touching. That creepy feeling inched up my spine again, seeing them together like that. When Kala finally got Pete to look at her, he had that killer grin on his face. And he looked . . . relieved.

"Earth to Ashley." Amber's voice knocked my head on straight.

"Sorry about that." I placed the phone back into view.

Amber sighed, taking a seat somewhere in a mall. "You in Minnesota yet?" I asked.

"Next week. Just picking up a few more things before making the trip."

Biting my lower lip, I glanced back to where Pete and Kala had walked down to make sure they weren't coming back. "Can I ask you something?"

"Yeah, you know you can ask me anything."

"What do you think of Pete? Honestly."

Her eyebrows raised. "You really want my honest answer?"

A scoff slipped from my mouth. "You'll give it to me no matter what."

"True." Amber glanced to the side before refocusing on me. "I don't know, Ash. I don't dislike Pete, but . . . "

"But what?"

"I've never seen someone fight for someone like that before. I'll give him that. But he's stupid as hell. I don't think he can handle a lot." Her eyes furrowed. "Meaning you."

I knew I could tell Amber anything, but my stomach was fluttering like crazy, bringing this up. I was nervous she'd judge me for the decisions I'd made during this trip. What was I thinking? Of course she would. Amber was my blatantly honest doppelgänger, and I loved her for it. Maybe that's why I was so nervous. Because I knew she'd give it to me straight when all I wanted to do was avoid it.

I shrugged. "I'm all messed up with him."

"You have been since you met him."

I sighed, chewing up my words. "I feel like I don't belong with him."

"Maybe you don't. You've been with so many shitty guys. But reality calling. Pete isn't the only un-shitty guy out there."

"I deserve them. The shitty guys."

"No one deserves the shitty ones. Not even you, Ash."

A smirk tickled the corner of my mouth. I glanced into the sky as Axel popped into my head.

"What's with that look?"

My attention went back to Amber. "What look?"

"Ash." Her lips puckered as she shook her head. "I know that look. What did you do?"

"Nothing!" My lips shut tight. "I . . . met this other guy."

"You met a guy? While on a trip with Pete?"

"Look. I told Pete no strings. He gets that."

Amber's eyes practically bulged out of her head. "See? If you really wanted to be with Pete, you wouldn't pull the benefits card. And this other guy, I mean, you're interested, right? Otherwise, you wouldn't look like you're up to no good."

"I guess so." My eyes shot back to the mountain. I could barely see the back of Pete's head. Kala was right against the tall standing gate, looking up at the presidential faces. Pete slowly came up behind her, laying a hand on her back.

My heart stopped in my chest. He didn't need to do that. It's not like she was going to fall. Heat rose to my face as my mouth twisted, trying to make logical sense of what I was seeing.

You said it was okay. Friends with benefits, remember?

But this feeling was anything but okay.

"So, who is this new guy?" Amber adjusted herself on the bench. "What's his name?"

She tore me from thinking about the *what if's* with Pete and quickly threw my mind into the *what if's* with Axel. "His name's Axel. He's been texting me on and off. You know, the guy who photobombed me. He's on a road trip, too."

I wasn't even sure if she heard what I said, but Amber took

another deep breath and really focused on the camera. "He looked more your type. Does he seem interested in you?"

"Yeah. He wants to see me again."

"So?" She shrugged. "See him again."

I leaned against one of the many flagpoles. "You think?"

"Ash, you are in a fucking tornado of shit right now. Seeing this guy seems like it's something you want. So, do what you want, right?"

"What about Pete?"

Amber sighed. "Do you love him?"

"What?"

"Do you *love* Peter?"

I slammed the back of my heels against the flagpole. "I'm scared . . . to be in love with Pete. One minute I want it so bad and the next I wanna run away from it."

"I know." There were a few tense moments of silence between us. Amber wasn't even looking at the camera as she thought of the next things to say. "I can't decide for you, Ash. But I have your back. Whatever you decide."

"Thanks, girl."

"You need a break from thinking. Maybe you need to be alone. I know you can't now, but when you get to California. Maybe that's what's best."

Thinking of letting Pete go was fucking scary. But which was scarier? Being with him or losing him. Or doing something stupid to mess it up. That was what I usually did. And I had a feeling I was trying to do it again. "This is so messed up."

"Everything is at some point." Amber gave a weary smile.

Another call buzzed my phone, causing my focus to spring loose. Axel's face flashed in the corner of my screen and my blood pressure skyrocketed. I'd been avoiding him like the plague, afraid of what smart-ass remark I would make to stir the pot more. Avoiding him forever wasn't an option. I could just tell him to screw off and be done with it. I had the balls to do it. But did I *want* to do it was the big question.

"I'm getting another call." I flashed a nervous smile.

"Is it this Axel guy?"

"Yeah. I've been kind of avoiding him."

"Don't let me stop you." Amber tightened her lip. "Love you, Ash."

A nerve-ridden sigh escaped through my teeth. "I know. Love you too. Talk to you later."

"Okay. Stay strong, girl."

I quickly swiped her off my screen, my finger lingering above his picture, unsure if I would ignore him or accept. Glancing back at the mountain, Pete and Kala were laughing about something, having a good ol' time. I needed this to get the thought of *them* out of my head. It didn't feel like I had pushed the green accept button, but soon he was there, looking at me from wherever he was.

"Hey, she lives." Axel's wavy dark locks were tucked under a bandana. He was sitting in the backseat of a car and it looked like he was on the road.

"Hey." My voice broke over my nerves and evened out. "Where are you now?"

"Leaving North Dakota and heading to Wyoming." He smirked. "Where have you been? You've been avoiding me, Harpy. I can see when you read my texts, you know."

"I haven't been . . . avoiding you."

"Oh really? Been busy?"

"Just . . . trying to figure my shit out."

"Well, while you're figuring your shit out, when can I see your pretty face again?"

My smile was too big to hide. Flirting was an addiction, and when someone started with me, I couldn't help myself. "You're looking at me now, aren't you?"

"Yeah, but nothing beats the real thing." His friends made some remarks which he shook his head at. He briefly left the screen to respond to them. I couldn't figure out what he was saying, but I didn't really care. "So," Axel smirked, "are you heading to Wyoming anytime soon?"

My lungs twisted in my chest. Old Faithful was our next stop after Mount Rushmore. And that was in Wyoming. Did I want to cross paths with Axel again? Did I want Pete to know about it? The answer to the first question was obvious. Yes, I wanted to see Axel again. He was chill and a looker and he seemed to like me. Those were all signs of something the old me loved to take advantage of. But Pete . . . fucking hell. Nothing was easy.

"Yeah, maybe we are."

"Well, well, well. Perhaps we can meet up? We're going to Devils Tower and spending the next few days camping out there."

"Oh, we're headed in the opposite direction."

Wyoming was big, and Old Faithful was west of Devils Tower. Like, incredibly west. As much as I relished in the knowledge of that, the old me begged to convince me otherwise.

"You could . . . not go opposite, right?"

"I don't know." Looking around, Pete or Kala were still talking it up, not noticing my absence. "I'd have to convince my sidekick."

"Well, convince him. Come to Devils Tower."

"Are you asking me or telling me?" I hung my head over my shoulder with a grin. "Because if you're telling me, you're barking up the wrong tree."

"I can't force you, obviously." Axel got closer to the camera. "And I think you like me barking up your tree."

"Fuck off, Ax."

"Ax?" He stifled a chuckle. "So, you *do* like me. What other nicknames have you thought about calling me?"

"Nothing you haven't already heard, I'm sure." My feet bounced against the pavement. I pushed away from the flagpole with a smile on my face. "All right, I'll keep you posted."

"I hope you do." He leaned back in the seat. "See you later, Harpy."

He hung up, leaving me to bask in the realization of what I had just done. Part of me was excited to get my old Ash on. Break the rules. Not give a shit. Just grab the bull by the balls in the moment. Axel was easy to like. He was the guy you'd ride an extreme coaster with. A rush without needing to think of what would happen if I let my hands fly up in the air and scream as loud as I could.

There was too much thinking involved with Pete. Maybe Amber was right. I needed a break from thinking.

twenty

. . .

south dakota, monday, august 10th

"OKAY, HERE'S ANOTHER ONE." Pete sat up in the back seat, shaking his head as if preparing for something.

Kala clung to the back of the passenger seat, her chin leaning against the headrest, keen to guess what Pete's next impression might be. I drove along the highway toward Wyoming, wondering what poor attempt at impersonation I was about to see.

Clearing his throat, Pete put on a serious face, furrowing his brow like he was about to throw down. "I have a bunch of questions." He spoke in an unusually thick accent. "And I want them answered immediately." He pointed to Kala, then at me, as I spied him in the rearview mirror. "Who is your daddy and what does he do?"

"Um," I shook my head, "what the hell are you doing?"

"It's not a tumor, *it's not a tumor!*" He kept on as we tried to debunk whoever it was he was trying to channel.

Kala stifled a laugh, glancing at me with a questioning look. "Um, you sound like the Terminator."

Pete shook his hands up and down. "Who is . . . "

"Wait, are you trying to be Arnold Schwarzenegger?" I asked.

"Oh my god, yes!" He fell back against the seat. "Wasn't it obvious?"

"No. What movie does he say, 'It's not a tumor?'"

"*Kindergarten Cop!* It's like his family friendly film, but with guns."

"A family friendly Schwarzenegger movie with guns?" I glanced at Kala, who only joined me in my obscure expression. "That's totally an oxymoron."

"*Jingle All The Way* was family friendly," Kala added. "So, it's possible."

"Yeah, but this was before that. The first attempt." Pete shrugged. "Obviously, they didn't quite hit the mark on family friendly. But still a classic."

"Sounds like a train wreck." I adjusted my sunglasses as we sped along the highway. It was mid-day, and the roads were a little more congested than usual. Not that it was unbearable.

"Okay, your turn, Ash." Kala sat forward in her seat.

"Nah, I'm driving. You take it for me."

"Okay." Kala folded her lips together, deep in thought. We were on day four of her riding with us since the wagon circle and no longer a guest, but an official crew-mate on our voyage. There hadn't been any more touching between her and Pete since Mount Rushmore. I hated thinking about it. And every time they so much as leaned toward each other, it came flooding back. But it gave me some time to figure out what I was doing. Maybe getting together with Axel wouldn't be so tragic after all.

"I got it." Kala sat back up in the seat, flipping her hair over her shoulder. "Only one is a wanderer. Two together are always going somewhere." Her voice was smooth and almost sensual.

Pete's attention perked, and he came away from the seat slowly. "No, I don't think that's necessarily true."

"Okay . . . " I cocked an eyebrow.

Shooting me a glance, Kala's dark eyes grew wide with embarrassment. "Oh, that's—"

"*Vertigo*, Kim Novak." Pete clapped his hands once. "One of Hitchcock's finest pieces of cinema." He breathed a sigh of nostalgia. "Can you quote that entire film?"

"Not all of it."

"Once again, you continue to impress me with your awesomeness, Kala."

Kala shrugged, tucking her dark hair behind her ear. "I don't know about that."

"What? No one said you're awesome before?"

"Not really."

"Well. I'm telling you." Pete raised his eyes up to catch her wandering gaze. "You're awesome."

Kala fell back in her seat, eyes shifting as she tried to hide the rising red of her cheeks. Pete took Gremlin out of his carrier and plopped him on his lap. He rubbed him behind the ears, which Gremlin accepted with blissfully closed eyes and a purr.

I kept my eyes on Pete through the rearview mirror. I didn't know if he was flirting or just trying to be nice. Was there a difference? He didn't seem overly stirred up, like flirting usually did to me. But that didn't mean it wasn't flirting.

Scrunching my mouth, there was no time like the present to ask him about Devils Tower. Plus, I was feeling a little rambunctious. I didn't want to assume, but there was no killing the whisper in the corner of my mind that he was deliberately trying to make me jealous. Getting back at me for all the shit I had put him through. If that was what it was, let him. Two could play at this game.

I wasn't nervous that Pete would say no to Devils Tower. It was me 'not planning on telling him the entire reason' after I promised I wouldn't keep things from him. But screw it, right? After seeing his hand on Kala and saying how awesome she was, the part that cared couldn't get a word in.

"Hey." I breathed. "Do you have your heart set on Old Faithful?"

"Yeah. It's a natural mall fountain. It sounds pretty epic to me." Pete looked up from his book. "Why? You not feeling it?"

I shrugged. "I don't know. Watching water shoot out of the ground doesn't sound that appealing."

"What else did you have in mind?"

I acted like I was thinking about where else I would want to whisk us away to. The name hung on the edge of my teeth for seconds, but it felt like hours. "What about Devils Tower?"

"There's a pretty cool legend about Devils Tower. And it's closer than Old Faithful," Kala chimed in.

"See?" I perked up. "It's right up your alley, then. A history lesson awaits you."

"I don't know." He went back to his comic. "I really wanted to see the geyser."

"We can stop on our way back to New York." I added in my vigilant attempt to change his mind. "Or while we're in California, take a weekend trip there."

"We can do that for Devils Tower, too."

My chest deflated as my hands settled on the wheel. "Think about it, okay?"

We were staying at a rinky-dink campground for the next two nights before making the final trek to Old Faithful or, hopefully, Devils Tower. Our site was open, staring out over a mountain scape of sorts, rolling down into a vast forest below. The sun was waning in the sky, a hint of twilight rustled through the trees and surrounding wildlife. Crickets were already chirping their heads off, adding to the music of the coming night.

Pete threw sticks and wood we had picked up at the campsite shop into the rounded fire pit. Kala was sitting in one of the lawn chairs we had packed, reading one of Pete's comic books. I kept watch at the kitchenette, stirring a pan filled with taco goodness.

A ton of '80s tunes were belting out of the camper speakers. Pete was in his element, bobbing his head to the music. He matched every lyric in perfect sync. He was being a complete dork, too adorable for words.

I stirred the skillet, letting the warm steam exfoliate my light brown skin. The weather wasn't too warm today, but I didn't need a jacket. However, I knew that I would need the fire as a heat source as soon as the sun went down.

Something disturbed Kala's reading, and she fished through her pockets to pull out her phone. "Hello?"

She sat quietly for a minute or two, her eyes shifting as someone spoke on the other line. She looked up at me for a second before returning her focus to what was being said. "Yeah. Okay." A pause. "I will. I love you too, Mom. I'll call you tomorrow." Kala stood. "Bye."

She put her phone back in her pocket with a sigh. With a raise of his forehead, Pete looked at her with keen suspicion. "Everything okay?"

A wave of relief flooded Kala's face. "Yeah. My mom talked to the police. That video you shot helped a ton. Since my parents have joint custody, my dad can't say I ran away. She said she asked you to bring me to California."

"Sweet! We're off America's Most Wanted for the time being." Pete clapped his hands. "This calls for marshmallows."

"After dinner!" I pointed my stirring utensil at him.

Just as I did, Whitney Houston's "Dance With Somebody" started ticking over the speaker. My ears perked up, letting out a woo in tandem with the song's intro.

"Well, if I have to wait. Might as well dance with somebody." I turned around as Pete started toward me.

Shaking my head, I couldn't help but smile as he grabbed me under my armpits and swung me around, a spoon still in hand. "No! Stop!" His arms captured me as he returned me to the ground, securing my waist as my hands fell across his shoulders. It's been a while since he held me like this. It was like everything that had happened that night in South Dakota erased from our memories. I couldn't stop smiling, leaking breathless giggles like a love-struck schoolgirl. His arms continued to support me as he whisked me around to the beat, never drawing away and never letting go.

I linked my hands together behind his neck, my hazel gaze pooling into his soft brown. As much as I didn't want him to stop, I had to remember I was trying not to fall. But I wanted to, even as the thought of deception crawled back into my mind.

"Ask Kala." I glanced at her after basking in the last steady seconds of bliss. "She needs to loosen up." My hands came away from his neck, trailing down to his chest. "I gotta finish dinner."

Pete's eyes shifted with a pang of disappointment. "You have a point there." His hands came off my waist, and he eyed Kala with playful intent.

Kala shook her head, sinking into her chair. "Oh, no. No, that's . . . it's okay. You don't have to."

"Nah, I think I do." Instead of barreling over to her, he was calm in his stride. Extending his hand with a slight bow. "May I?"

"No. It's okay. I don't dance." Kala moused away as she looked up at him.

"Maybe you just haven't found the right dance partner." Pete took her hand. "Come on, it'll be fun."

Pulling her off the chair, Pete caught her surprised expression as he slid one arm around her waist, taking her hand in the other. "Is this okay?"

Kala was tense out of the chair but soon relaxed, resting her hands on his shoulders. "Yeah. It's okay."

Whitney's smash hit winded down and The Cure's "Friday" followed soon after it. I smiled as I watched Pete take her around the fire pit, each step making her more and more comfortable. Soon, she was laughing and smiling at Pete's twists and twirls as he took her across the entire campsite to the music.

I stirred the food slowly, listening to it pop and spark from the heat. He didn't even try to argue with me. He went for Kala without seeming the least bit regretful. And Kala . . . her feelings were so clear that it made my skin crawl. She was falling for him. How could she not? After I told her I wasn't with Pete and this was just a fling. She didn't need to be careful.

I had to know if he was falling too or it would turn me into the most ugly version of myself. A person even Pete hadn't seen.

twenty-one

. . .

south dakota, monday, august 10th

THE SKY WAS like a light splattered scene over a dark canvas. It was insane to think how small we were in a universe so big. People who didn't believe in life outside of our own planet were bogus.

After dinner and countless s'more roasting, we laid out a plaid blanket over the ground. Pete lay in between Kala and I, an arm behind his head, eyes fixed on the spectacular light show above us. I couldn't see if he was holding Kala's hand, but the logical side of my brain told me he wouldn't be that bold.

I'd never see stars like this in New York. Maybe upstate, but nothing like this. Kala was wearing a plaid sweat jacket, and I had on my Pink Floyd sweatshirt Pete had gotten me when were in Ohio.

Music pulsed from Pete's phone, but it was low, so low it melted with the sounds of the night.

"This is crazy," Pete breathed. "The amount of stars out there. Suns. Some with their own planets spinning around them. Mind blowingly crazy."

"Yeah," I agreed. A memory popped into my head. I was six or seven and my dad had taken my brothers and me on a camping trip to the Catskills. A tiny cabin in the middle of the mountains with a killer flat roof for stargazing. He took us out there one night, hot chocolate in our thermoses, telling us stories he had heard as a kid about the Aboriginal's living in the bush. He'd walk around us as we sat huddled together, arms outstretched, enthusiasm and passion dripping from his lips. Even at that age, he was immortal.

"What's on your mind?"

I came back to the present. Turning to my left, I saw Pete watching me curiously.

"Oh, nothing." I glanced down at the fine threads lacing the blanket together. "I mean," I looked back toward the sky. "Just old memories resurfacing."

"Your dad?" he spoke calmly, knowing how touchy the subject of my dad was. I couldn't even believe I had said anything at all about what I was thinking, softening up to it more and more.

"Yeah. He loved telling us stories about shit like this. The stars." I glanced at him.

"My Unci too," Kala added, without taking her eyes from the sky. "When I was a kid."

"Unci means?" Pete asked.

"Grandfather." She settled her hands across her stomach. No hand holding. That kept my insanity at bay for the moment. "We're connected to the stars. Every child born possesses *wanagi*, or a star spirit. They stay with us our whole lives and when we die, our *wanagi* is taken into the sky."

"What happens then?" Pete asked, genuinely intrigued by the story she wove.

"It travels to the *Wicakiyuhapi*, taken by the carriers on a blanket to cross the bridge of the Milky Way." She glanced at us. "*Wicakiyuhapi* are the stars of the Big Dipper. And the blanket is the cup. Then it travels down the handle to return to the space beyond."

Silence crept upon us as the last words of her settled in the night. "There's a saying the Lakota use, '*Mitakuye Oyasin*'. It means all my relations. Most people don't understand that it doesn't mean just the families we are born into, but every living thing that ever was. We all come from the stars. All born from the sky."

"Shit," I whispered. "That's pretty intense to think about."

"Yeah. Intense." Pete shifted on the blanket, bringing his hands to his chest.

We continued our silent stargazing, letting thoughts and dreams swarm like fireflies in our minds. It was humbling to think that when my dad died; he returned to the stars. Or became something else. He always liked birds. Maybe he was one, soaring through the sky, seeing the world from an entirely new perspective.

"I'm gonna go to bed." Kala sat up, stretching her arms out with a wide yawn.

Pete popped himself up on his elbows as she moved to stand. "Snuggle the crap out of Gremlin."

"Okay. Good night, guys."

She slipped off the blanket and walked past the fire pit to the camper. "Maybe I should turn in too."

"No." Pete's hand grasped my arm. "Can you stay?"

I should have pulled away, but I couldn't. It was rare we had a moment to ourselves since Kala had been with us. Talking or just being together. "Okay."

Before I could lie back down, he slid his arm under me, pulling me against him to settle in the crux of his arm. His shirt was cool, having absorbed the night air. I closed my eyes as I lay against him, taking in his summer scent. The gentle rise and fall of his chest should have brought me a sense of peace, but it only left me anxious. I hated how much I was fighting against the current with him. Karate chopping the waves as they tried to suck me under and just accept how much I wanted to belong with him.

"How have you been, honestly?" His question lingered in the air as I kept my eyes fixed on the profile of him. I rested my hand on his chest, the gentle beating of his heart sending my stomach twisting into countless knots.

"I don't know. Guess I'm okay." I press closer against him. "I'm just trying to take it a step at a time."

"Kala's a pleasant distraction from everything."

I lift my head to brandish my grin to him. "For you or me?"

"Both. It's not as tense with her here. It's kind of nice."

Some minimal truth exposed. He liked Kala being around. So did I. He dragged his fingers across my hand, my bracelet mildly breaking the pattern of his light touch. "I noticed you put this back on."

I recoiled my fingers into my palm as he continued to trace along my skin. "Yeah." I shrugged against him. "It carried too much pain, and I tried to bury it. Another lie I forced myself to believe I could live without."

"Is it—"

"My dad's." I settled his curiosity before he assumed. "It's from my dad."

He grasped my fist. "What changed?"

I let my mouth hang open as I tried to piece together words that made sense. "Realizing I can't just bury shit and forget it ever existed."

We lingered for a moment, eyes cast to the stars. Even though we were on top of each other, I felt disconnected. Like it wasn't me lying in the nook of Pete's arm, feeling his hand on mine. Maybe I was becoming desensitized from it or I realized how much I longed to feel that connection with him again.

His hand came up, slipping a few strands of hair from polluting my face. "It's hard, you know. Keeping myself from you."

I shifted my gaze; the truth sinking me deeper into my hole of indecisiveness. "I wish you didn't have to."

He sat up, making sure I moved with him. "Then tell me. Right now. Tell me not to hold back."

I shook my head. "I don't know if I can."

"Why not?"

I shrugged as I tried to come up with an answer. Because I wanted to see Axel. Because I think I'm wrong about you. Because I think Kala is crushing on you. Nothing sounded right, even though all of it was true.

His lips tightened as he held his breath. "Stop making excuses, Ash. Stop refusing to move on with your life."

I pulled away from him, laying my hands on my lap. "I wish I was a better person for you."

"You are." He sat up, taking my face in his hands. "You're beautiful." And then he kissed me, so full of ferocity that the force of it took me aback.

He kept me against him as I clung to his arms, the sweet watermelon taste of him calming the chaos from my mind as we remained together. Our kiss deepened, rising and falling against my racing heart. When he finally drew away, I looked into his eyes, knowing what he would say next without him even needing to say it.

"I love you, Ashley Carter." His hands fell into mine. "The only one making this hard is you."

He moved to leave, but I tightened my grip on his arms. "Pete, wait."

He looked back at me as Joy Division drifted to my ears; the atmosphere sending memories of our first dance together on the baseball field flooding into my eyes. Memories that could have meant more if I could just let go.

"It's our song," I whispered. "Will you dance with me?"

He lingered, wrestling with his pain and desire all at the same time. But he pulled me up and held onto my waist while I stared into his hopelessness. My arms went around his neck, pressing my forehead against his as he kept me close. I closed my eyes and let the lyrics invade my mind.

I wish I could go back to that night on the baseball field. I had been a mess then, but in all the best ways. He had swept me off my feet. Carried me into a feeling I never thought I'd be worthy of experiencing. Nerves shot into my heart, exhausted from longing. I wish I had kissed him then. It would have been perfect. So perfect I would have told Wes to fuck off and that would have been the end. But I hadn't.

And now, as much as I never wanted to let him slip away once the song came to a close, I could feel how heavy this was. Not weightless and free like on the baseball field, but riddled with toxicity. Poison that I injected willingly and without retaliation. This already felt hopeless, despite how much he said he loved me. I felt the same way about him, but was too afraid it wasn't real. That he really was falling for Kala and I really wasn't good enough. How could I take that chance knowing all the chances I had taken in the past chewed me up and spit me out every time?

Even Ian Curtis' lyrics were telling me not to walk away. Like he knew I would be here. Under the stars. Maybe he was here, too. Watching from above. Realizing the storm we were in before anyone else was aware of it.

twenty-two

· · ·

wyoming, wednesday, august 12th

SINCE THAT NIGHT, I couldn't get what Pete had said out of my head. He had been right, like always. I was the one making it difficult.

We left the campsite early the following day, stopping at a gas station before heading to Old Faithful. I stood outside the car, my hand on the gas pump, staring at the numbers as they filled the tank. Each tick bringing me closer or further from where I wanted to be.

I couldn't bring up Devils Tower again. Fuck it. I couldn't do it. Axel was a mistake, a taste of the old me I thought I needed to quench. He texted me to ask if my convincing antics worked, but I didn't answer. I let it hang, just like I was leaving him.

"I'm gonna grab some snacks." Pete walked around the car to head toward the picturesque mid-western style gas station convenient store. "Want anything?"

I shook my head, rendering a weak smile. I was glad I had my shades on so he wouldn't see how much I was struggling.

Kala leaned out of the passenger side window. "Get me a red slush if they have?"

Pete pointed to her. "A lady after my heart. You got it." He walked off, entering the store through the chiming doors.

Kala leaned on her folded arms, watching me stare at nothing and thinking about everything. "Can I tell you something?"

Glancing at her, I keep a firm hand on the pump. "Yeah."

Kala hesitated, looking back at the store like Pete would come out and ruin what she was about to say. "I wasn't eavesdropping, but I saw you two. Kissing. But it was sad. Like a kiss goodbye." Her head came off her arms. "Pete really likes you. I would kill for a guy like him. He's funny and smart and kind. He listens and is so understanding. How do you not see that?"

The pump stopped with a full tank. I stared at it, leaving it tethered to the car without releasing it. "I see it."

"Then what are you doing?"

"Fucking it up." I pulled the pump from the car.

"Does he make you happy?"

I turned to her with the pump in hand. "Does he make *you* happy?"

Kala's mouth grew thin. I had caught her feeding the dog under the table. I bit my tongue, keeping myself from saying anything else. The ugly Ash was standing behind my teeth, slowly squeezing through the cracks to rip this girl a new asshole. I didn't want to be that person. Not to her. It wasn't her fault. None of this was.

Rushing footsteps approached the car, and Pete hopped over the curb. "Hey, here's your slush. As requested." Pete handed Kala her giant drink. "You okay?"

Kala squinted, forcing a smile as she took the drink. "Thanks, Pete." She looked back at me, slowly melting into the passenger's seat, before placing the straw in her mouth to occupy her thoughts.

I replaced the pump in its holster. Pressing yes to get the receipt printed. Pete came over to me, his arm touching my shoulder. "Mind if I drive?"

I tensed for a minute before loosening my tongue. "Sure, I don't mind."

"Good. I wanna make sure you don't change your mind about Devils Tower."

I couldn't breathe as my head shot to him. "Pete, we don't have to."

"But you want to. So, we'll go." He moved to head back to the car, but I grabbed his shirt, keeping him there.

"Pete," I muttered, "I need to talk to you."

"Later, okay? When we get there. So, it's just you and me." His smile stuffed cotton down my throat, leaving me without words of retaliation. "I promise."

I let go of him, turning back toward the pump. The receipt flapped in the wind. A dry smell suffocating me even further into the Devils oblivion.

"Shit," I whispered as I yanked the receipt free. "Shit. Shit. Shit."

twenty-three

. . .

wyoming, wednesday, august 12th

I DIDN'T KNOW where Axel would be. Devils Tower was gigantic. It would be like finding a needle in a haystack. And Axel didn't know where we would be. So I had nothing to worry about.

But it was still hanging on my mind the entire car ride, leaving me practically catatonic. I kept my headphones on, staring out the window in my headspace. Pulling the "not feeling well" card worked for now, but I could tell Kala knew it wasn't the whole truth. She was careful, more stand-offish in her conversation with Pete. I watched them, not entirely knowing what they were talking about because of the music blasting in my ears. She caught my eye every now and again, and she looked worried. Worried with a secret.

Gremlin sat in my lap, purring and letting me rub his chin into blissful awareness. At least there was one guy I wouldn't have to worry about losing.

The closer we got to Devils Tower, the worse the knots in my stomach became. They tightened and tensed up my ribcage, yanking at my lungs and keeping my body rigid.

When the giant rock formation crested the highway's horizon, I felt like dying. This was typical of how the events of my life played out. I decided I would go one way and something pulled me in the other direction. Or landed at my feet and kept me from taking the decisive step forward.

The car bumped into the national park, and Pete came up to the booth to secure a campsite. Muffled voices spoke, but I ignored what they said. I put the volume of my headphones to max, keeping Kate Bush's "Running Up That Hill" flooding my mind as the truth of her words pierced my heart.

We made for the site. It was early evening, and the sun was slowly dropping to the horizon. Pete backed the camper into our temporary home. The trees created a cozy nook on either side, framing a breathtaking view of the flat land that rolled beneath the tower. It was so big, I wouldn't be able to escape it, even if I tried.

Must be karma.

I didn't feel like doing much when we got there. Pete and Kala lit a fire while I crawled into the camper. Curling up with a blanket and my headphones, I went over in my head what I would say to Pete once we sat down to talk. All I wanted to do was disappear. Run up the tower and never come back down.

I twisted my bracelet around my wrist. It was heavy. So heavy I thought my hand would fall off. I enjoyed the burden, like some sick, obsessed drug addict. I wanted it to be heavier, so I could forget to feel and just let things happen without caring.

There was a knock on the camper door. I pulled myself up from the bed, my hair shifting from one side to the next. "What?"

Kala opened the door and slid onto the bed quietly. After taking off her shoes, she turned to look at me, her hands folded in her lap. "How are you feeling?"

I stared at her, wanting so badly to yell at her. Maybe I would. Because I didn't know what else to do at this point. Everything I wanted contradicted the other things I wanted. Nothing made sense anymore.

"Don't worry about me," I tried to say calmly, but knew my tone wasn't entirely without remorse.

"Look." She licked her lips before pressing them firmly together. "I wanted to say something—"

"That you like Pete?" I sucked in a harsh breath. "Sorry. That you're *falling* for Pete, I should say."

"What?" Kala shook her head. "No. I mean . . . I do like Pete, but—"

"You don't have to lie to me, Kala. I'm not stupid."

"I never said you were." She squinted. "Why are you so angry?"

My phone buzzed on the overhead shelf, but I didn't feel like answering. In case it was Axel. "Just tell me why you came in here, then fuck off, okay? I don't want to be bothered right now."

Kala's lips tightened, holding back the emotion my brashness left her with. "I just wanted to, you know, I would never do anything to hurt you. You're . . . you're my friend and . . . " She looked down at her hands, now pressed firmly against her thighs. "I didn't have any friends before meeting you, Ash. You and Pete." She looked at me. "You're it."

Fuck me.

Her eyes shimmered with tension-built tears she refused to let out. "I . . . just wanted you to know that." She slid back to the door. "I'll leave you alone now."

I watched her open the door and grab her shoes without bothering to put them on. It silenced me into a black hole. When the door finally closed, I threw myself back against the bed. I was a terrible person.

My phone rang again, and by the third time, I finally reached for it.

Dimitri.

I clicked accept.

"Sis, where have you been? I've been calling you all day." He sounded playful but annoyed, worry in every word.

"Sorry. I haven't been feeling good."

"You sick?"

"No. I'm . . . not really. There's just a lot of shit going on."

There were a few seconds of silence. I wasn't sure if I was about to confess everything or sweep it under the rug like I always did.

Memories of our last conversation came flooding back. He wanted me to confide in him. But it was so hard to push myself to do it.

"Where you at now?" he asked, his tone less exacerbated.

"Wyoming. We just got to Devils Tower."

"How's it going with Pete? You two getting along, okay?"

A wave of chills threatened the nervous nausea in my stomach. "I don't know. I think I messed up."

"What happened?"

I was afraid to tell him because of what he would think. Dimitri and I lost the connection we had after my dad died because of me. But what he thought of me still mattered. I needed someone to look to more than ever. As much as I wished it were my dad, it couldn't be. Dimitri was all I had.

"I've been pushing him away and . . . " I didn't expect myself to get emotional, but tears soon leaked from my face onto the blanket wrapped around me. "We came here because a guy I met on the road asked me to. Pete doesn't know and . . . I didn't think we'd come. But he said yes; and now I'm afraid he'll find out."

Dimitri cleared his throat. "Does this other guy know you're there?"

"No. I was gonna call it off. Since he asked, I haven't spoken to him. I don't want to be here, but . . . I've already screwed so much shit up. Pete . . . he'll never come back." My voice cracked as I closed my eyes to my confession. The blatant immaturity of this entire thing was shameful to me. All I wanted was to break free from my past mistakes, but I kept falling back into them. Again and again.

I wasn't able to catch my breath. I was searching for anything to help me cope with this unnatural surge of emotions.

"Ash," Dimitri spoke, "take a deep breath. Try to calm down."

"What am I gonna say?" I blubbered out.

"The truth. Tell him the truth."

"I can't."

"Why?"

I held my breath before letting it leak out slowly through my mouth. "Because I'm gonna lose him if I do."

"Ash." Dimitri sighed. "You made your bed. Now you gotta lie in it."

"D . . . "

"Nah. I'm giving you the hard truth. Someone has to. You love this dude, right?"

I hesitated, sniffling loudly as I settled into the blanket. "Yeah. I do."

"How would you feel if someone you loved did this to you? What would you have wanted them to do?"

Witnessing the connection Kala had with Pete was agonizing beyond measure. Jealousy was killing me inside. I didn't believe Kala wasn't falling for Pete, but I knew she meant it when she said she didn't want to hurt me. "I'd want them to be honest."

"So, this is me. Being honest with you. I don't want you to hurt, but life is full of hard lessons. This is one of yours. Whatever happens, you got me in your corner. But I'm not gonna coddle you through it. Because that's not how life works."

My eyes closed, and I quietly nodded as if he could see me. "Okay."

"So, do it before it eats you alive. No matter what the outcome is, you did the right thing. The honest thing. And that's all you can do."

Fear wasn't the right word. Petrified, maybe. Nothing scared me more than telling Pete how much I regretted all the bullshit I'd pulled on him this entire trip. He wanted to be with me. But I was a tease. A full on *Breakfast Club* Claire. Someone I both despised and admired.

Yeah, I adored my bitchy side. Used it as my power move again and again. But it had also wounded me knowing how many people I'd hurt because of it. How it left me riddled with scars.

"Ash." Dimitri's voice pulled me out of my head. "You can do this."

"Okay." I shut off the waterworks and looked out of the skylight. Stars were already twinkling in the sky. The flickering firelight still pulsed through the glass. "Okay."

"I'm sorry . . . I left you behind. God, I regret it every fucking day, even though I had to. But I'm here now."

"I know." My eyes closed; I wanted nothing more than to be

squeezed by Dimitri's linebacker biceps as I cried all over him. "I know you are."

The bracelet eased on my wrist. It felt good clearing the air with Dimitri. Knowing that, even though I carried this burden, he was there to encourage me to stand when I fell. And I would fall. So many times. But it was required.

The fall was part of moving on. It was the only way I could build the strength to push myself up. And every time I fell, it would be easier to stand. Without needing someone to catch me. Without needing to be afraid to fall.

twenty-four

· · ·

wyoming, thursday, august 13th

THE NEXT MORNING, I got up early. There was no way I could talk to Pete after getting off the phone with Dimitri. I had to be composed and not let anything distract me from what I needed to say. It was impossible to sleep. Going over the script in my head I was preparing for Pete. I didn't know how many times I could use the word 'stupid', but it was probably not nearly as many as it should have been.

I must have looked like shit, but I didn't care. Throwing on my sweatshirt and a pair of tight Bermuda shorts, I slipped on my hiking boots and stepped out of the camper, making sure not to wake Kala. It was slightly cool as the sun tickled through the leaves. I tied my uncombed mop of hair into a bun, feeling the heaviness of swollen bags under my eyes.

I took a deep breath in, holding it in my lungs with my eyes closed. Dad's voice slipped through my ears and flooded my senses. *"Nothing can happen until you take the first step."*

Breathe in. Breathe out.

The anxiety subsided enough for me to get over the boulder of my doubts and grab water from our mini fridge. As I approached the back of the car where Pete had been sleeping since Kala joined us, I knocked on the window, watching him stir until he woke up.

"Oh, hey." He rubbed his eyes. "You're up early. Feeling better?"

"No. I need to talk to you." I tucked the water bottle in the pocket of my sweatshirt. "Can you take a walk with me?"

He sat up. "Like this?" He was wearing a plain white tee and boxers, but I didn't care if he was butt naked.

The longer I waited, the harder it would be to get my words out. If I needed to be pushy, then so be it. "Get dressed, then. I'll wait."

He grabbed his glasses as I stepped away from the car to let him get dressed. I couldn't keep my feet still. Molten rock burned through my veins, and my heart was about to explode.

Pete came up next to me. "Okay, I'm as ready as I'll ever be." He pointed to the fridge. "Just let me grab some OJ and we can go."

We walked through the campsite, finding a trail that led into the wilderness. Devils Tower was creeping up on us. Its massive size only continued to grow with each step. The wind blew through the plains with such force it made the open space feel even more vast.

Pete kept glancing at me again and again, waiting for me to say my piece. But I was stuck with it, and the more we walked, the tougher it got to say what had to be said.

"So," he looked around, the sun reflecting on his glasses, "did you really wanna talk or did you just want an excuse to get me out here alone to kill me?"

I didn't look up, not feeling anything but anxious. "No, I wanted to talk."

"Okay. So. Talk."

Coming up a hill, the trail turned east, overlooking a small outcrop of flat land and hills. I wondered if the air had always been like this, or maybe I was finally noticing how refreshing it was. Like a lot of other things. "You know when you said I was the one making things hard?"

"Yeah."

My legs seized, head still down, as I tried to face him. "You were right."

A pinch in my spine forced me to look at him. It was my conscious finally holding me accountable for all the bullshit. Now I was ready to deal with it and leave the old me behind. "I don't want to make it hard anymore."

Pete watched me, his expression unconvinced. I'd practically trained him to be cautious at this point. "What do you mean by that?"

"I mean," my feet moved toward him with a weary step, "no more bullshit. No more circles. I've been stringing you along even though I said no strings. And I'm sorry."

Devils Tower loomed above me, casting an eerie shadow, making me feel uneasy. But I'm through with the shadow that held me back. Forget all that doubt for what it convinced me to do, and screw me for listening for so long.

Again, my eyes shifted. "I wanna try. To be here for you." I met his eyes again. "Just you."

His lips went thin, his head dropping to his feet as they closed the gap between us. "You're serious?" Brown eyes rejoined my hazel. "You're not gonna change your mind tomorrow?"

I shook my head. "This is me changing my mind. I want this." His hands folded into mine. "I want you."

"Damn." A nervous breath escaped him. "You don't know how long I've wanted to hear you say that."

I couldn't wait any longer, so I grabbed him, the tangy acid of the orange juice still present on his lips. His hands slipped around my waist, keeping me close to prolong the inevitable. I'd never felt so fucking light. Like I was floating on a cloud or whatever people compare this feeling with.

Nothing constricted me, no memories of my mistakes or regrets of what should have been. It might have taken me months to get my head on straight, but at least I had.

And it wasn't too late.

My arms came around him, deepening the meaning I'd put behind this everlasting kiss. I wanted him to feel like it was real. That this was legit, the path I wanted. He felt so good. His arms around me and his taste coating my tongue.

Drawing away was the worst thing, but I leaned my head against his forehead, nestling my nose over his glasses, causing them to shift against his face.

"I didn't know how much longer I could wait." His arms tightened around me. "I wanted to, but it was . . . so fucking hard."

"I was foolish and I'm sorry. I'm so sorry." My face burrowed into his shoulder, keeping him as close to me as I could. He breathed in my spearmint scent, running his hands up my spine with a final exhale.

My heart was beating so fast, my head was spinning. I was so weak for him.

But then I saw, coming up the path, three bodies of unwelcomed familiarity. My blood turned cold. I had to tell him. I had to tell him now. "Pete." I drew away from him, keeping my arms on his shoulders. "I have something to tell you."

"What?"

My hands fell to his, and I grabbed them tightly, the panic rising my throat. "Coming here. It was—"

"Hey, Harpy!"

Our eyes shot to Nate, Curtis, and Axel as they came traipsing up the hill. They all had their backpacks and hiking boots on. Axel with a bandana tied around his head. "You made it."

"Made it?" Pete dropped my hands in an instant, stepping away like I had the plague.

"Pete, I—"

"Glad you convinced him to come." Axel and his friends stopped once they got closer to the scene that was about to boil over. "Or . . . maybe you . . . didn't?" Axel's hand went to the back of his neck.

"No." Pete glanced at him before seething back at me. "No, she failed to mention *the reason*."

"I was gonna tell you."

"Was that before or after? Because before would have been nice."

"Later, dude." Both Nate and Curtis slipped past us. "Not getting caught in this."

Axel moved to pass us as well, but he lingered just before the turn.

I took a desperate step toward Pete, but he moved away from me. "Can you just listen, please?"

"You knew he'd be here. That's why you wanted to come? For him?"

Words stuck in my throat like glue. "Yes. At first, but—"

"But nothing, Ash!"

"I didn't think you'd say yes. I wanted to call it off, but . . . was afraid to tell you why."

"So, you sat there and let it happen?" His brows raised. "Like you thought that would be better?"

"I don't . . . I don't know."

"I am such an idiot." He threw his hands up. "Do whatever the fuck you want." He turned back down the hill.

Lunging forward, I grabbed his arm, forcing him to turn. "Please don't go. I meant what I said."

"So did I." He yanked his arm away. "Enjoy your no strings, Ash. And don't follow me."

His harsh eyes flashed to Axel. "She's all yours."

And he was gone, storming down the hill back toward the campground. My legs were glued to the ground, even with the scorching mid-west heat. It boiled inside of me like a hot oven. The amount of stupidity I could pull was unfathomable. Dimitri was right; I was lying in my bed now. And there wasn't anything I could say to make it right.

My hands landed on my head as I reeled back to project into the sky, *"Fuck!"* As much as I wanted to run after him, I knew it wouldn't make a difference. I just had to wait for him to cool off.

"I'm sorry, Harpy." Axel's voice crept up behind me. "Sounds like bad timing. Or perfect timing."

"I don't need your *bullshit* right now." I breathed, dropping my arms and turning around. "Please, just go away."

He glanced up the hill. "Why don't you come with? We have plenty of food for the hike."

"No, thanks." Leaving the situation like this with Pete ate away at my core, but I didn't want to push him more over the edge than I already had. Hanging with Axel felt like another slap to the face. No matter what I did, it would be the wrong decision.

"Come on. It'll clear your head." His dark eyes flashed. "That dude needs space, anyway. Even if you wanted to talk to him, he'd blow you off."

I wanted to scream at myself. To kick and throw punches at the trees till my knuckles bled. I couldn't be so reckless anymore.

But there was Axel, holding out a hand to pull me out. A gesture I told myself I would avoid from now on. But it was so welcoming. So unbelievably easy to just reach out and take it.

"Fine." I huffed and turned back up the hill, taking the hand of temptation.

twenty-five

. . .

wyoming, thursday, august 13th

IT WAS a long hike up that I wasn't prepared for. But I needed to feel the burn in my legs and feet. Sweat dripped down my back, even with my sweatshirt off and tied around my waist. The only things I wished I had were Pete and my shades, though maybe the glare was good for me. It exposed me to the emotional fire I finally stopped feeding. But it was still burning, not ready to go out.

The guys left me alone mostly, bickering and goofing off. Axel would look back every once in a while. He offered to hold my water and gave me a PowerBar. But other than that, he let me be. It was refreshing being surrounded by new company. I think it was the pressure. Pressure to think one thing but do something entirely different.

I meant what I said. I wanted to be with Pete. And it sucked, feeling like I had no control over it. I didn't know why I thought I ever had control over anything.

We reached a family of rocks and boulders decorating the edge of a cliff. There was a shady spot where a few branches offered a break from the sun. Sliding into one, I deflated with a long, drawn-out breath. My eyes wandered over the scene laid out in front of me. It wasn't until this trip that I realized how big this world was. New York was the concrete jungle, but this . . . this was the ocean. Endless and without limits.

"Here." Axel sat down next to me, my water bottle in his hand.

"Thanks." I took it and chugged it down. I was not dressed for a hike. My tank top was soaked with sweat and my skin was shining like a wet rock.

Axel rubbed his shoulders under his Wu-Tang tank, his bandana keeping the sweat from pouring down his forehead. His hair was remarkably stable, but a little muffled. "Doing okay?"

A loud huff escaped through my nose. "No. But I rarely am."

"Relationships suck." He pulled out his water bottle and downed a few gulps, his Adam's apple bobbing up and down with each chug. He gave a satisfying exhale as he parted from the spout. "That's why I avoid them."

"Like, completely?"

He shrugged. "Well, I try anyway." His gaze fell out over the landscape. "My dad was real shitty. Used to beat up on my mom. Until I grew up and I beat up on him."

"Shit." A pang of familiarity crept over my bones.

"I got juvy for a few months. When I got out, my mom wised up. Left him. And we moved to California." He smirks, glancing at me. "Some origin story, right?"

"Definitely not anything to bat an eye at." I put my water bottle on the rock beside me. "Sorry you had to deal with that."

Axel shrugged. "I'm not. It was a hard lesson. I never want to see that bastard again. And yeah, it left its scars." He shook his head. "I try not to show them off too much."

"What was the longest relationship you've ever been in?"

He curled his mouth, casting his eyes in thought. "Like . . . an actual relationship?" He shook his head. "I'm more of a weekender. Maybe four days tops."

"Wow." I practically chuckled. "That long, huh?"

"Well, this one with Pete just lasted ten seconds for you, so I think I got you beat."

My hand came off the rock, ready to strike, but I recoiled, nodding my head through gritted teeth. "I guess you do."

He noticed my tension and leaned to one side. "Sorry. Didn't mean to strike a fresh wound." He dropped his head before finding my eyes again. "How long have you not *not* been with him?"

I leaned on my left hand. "What's that supposed to mean?"

Axel took another long swig of his water bottle. "He's into you. I mean, it's obvious by how pissed he was. And you," he licked any stray drops from his lips. "seem like you are too."

"Yeah, well. I'm a class A screw up."

"Everyone screws up."

"Not as often as me. Or as purposefully." Breathing a sigh, I continued to gaze over the open landscape.

"Hey." Curtis' voice drew both mine and Axel's attention. "We're gonna head back. You coming?"

Axel looked at me before turning back to his friend. "Gonna hang a little longer."

"All right, meet you back there."

"Later." Nate waved and the two of them headed back toward camp.

Axel waited for them to disappear before turning back to me. "So, what's your plan, then?"

I raised an eyebrow. "Plan for what?"

"For what you're gonna do once this pleasant hike has concluded?"

The corner of my mouth twitched. "Do I look like a girl with a plan?"

He cracked a charming smile. "Same. A plan? Not me." He leaned back, stretching his legs out in front of him. "Nah, I'd rather just go with the flow."

"Is that why your relationships only last four days?"

"That's harsh." He sucked in air through his teeth, dropping his legs back against the rock. "There was one girl." He chuckled to himself. "I couldn't quit her. For a while, I was like a lost puppy, you know? Ending up at her doorstep every night."

"What happened?" I came up with my hands and settled them in my lap, genuinely interested in a relationship that didn't involve me.

"She just wasn't the one, I guess. Not that I think that exists."

"You don't believe in just one guy, one girl? Lasting forever?"

"No way. That shit's a fairy tale."

I dropped my gaze to my hands, my thumbs rubbing the creases of my skin. Love like that was real. Maybe it was a fairy tale to some people, and that was sad. But my parents had it. I saw it every day they were together. I never remembered them fighting or disagreeing on anything, except maybe what was for dinner. Even those were mixed with laughter and soft touches of affection. It was beautiful to witness. Sometimes I think it was a miracle I came from that love, knowing all the mistakes I'd made and the rotten relationships I'd found myself in. If there was anything more that I wanted, it was love like that. And I found it. And I was squandering it. "I'm not so sure."

The sounds of birds singing in the trees masked the quiet between us. A sudden drop in my stomach forced me to hold my breath. Not just from the sweat of the hike, but something on the inside.

This didn't feel right.

Axel took another swig of his water before replacing it in his backpack. "That girl made my heart stop every time I saw her." I felt his dark eyes on me. "Kind of like you."

"Pfft." I smiled, leaning away from him. "Is that what you tell all the girls you meet?"

He flashed his teeth with that charm of his. "Only the ones I want to stick around."

"What? You think we'd last more than a weekend?"

Axel shrugged, that wickedly dangerous smirk cutting across his face. "Can't say for sure. Maybe." He looked out into the wilderness. "Out here, anything is possible."

"I thought you didn't believe in that shit?"

He shrugged and looked at me. "Prove me wrong, then."

I stared at him, trying to figure out what the hell it was that made me want to act on my impulses. Let go of the person I was trying to become and tear down all the work I had put into myself to change. Through his words and cunning charm, I felt special. Like how Wes made me feel when he found me deflated, drowning in my own self destruction. He flirted with me because he wanted me. Wanted it to be just us and let go of all the unwanted baggage I had been carrying.

When I did, he became the only thing keeping me together. And when he fell apart, I didn't know how to let him go. Because if I did, I would fall right back into that pit of despair he pulled me from. I depended on him for everything. That was my mistake. And I was making it again, right now. Riding the waves of my feelings.

Pete taught me to climb out of that darkness using only my own two hands. I didn't need anyone to make me feel special. No one could make me feel anything unless I allowed them to control my life. That was what this had been about. Control. To me, commitment meant I was releasing control of my life and it petrified me to let that happen again.

But that was backward. That wasn't what genuine commitment was. Not the commitment that Pete had for me.

I slid off the rock, knowing I had to get back to Pete as soon as I could. "I'm ready to go back now."

"All right, Ash." He came off the rock and faced me. "Now that I know your name, am I allowed to use it?"

"I don't know." I grinned, leaning my head to one side. As irresistible as Axel was, I had to stop this, and I couldn't do it in the old Ash way.

"Well then, lead the way, Harpy."

twenty-six

. . .

wyoming, thursday, august 13th

WALKING BACK, it had to be mid-afternoon. I left my phone at the campsite so I could focus on telling Pete how I felt. At least, that was the idea.

We were covered in sweat by the end of the trail. I could use a shower. I probably stank like dirty gym socks.

Going down sideways, I braced myself as I descended the slope. I guess I was more tired than I thought because I stumbled, tripping over my feet and sliding down on my butt.

I guess that was one way of doing it.

"You okay?" Axel jumped down, landing too perfectly beside me as I wiped the dirt from my skidded hands.

"Yeah." I swiped the settled dust from my face. "I'll live."

"Here." He grabbed my arm, pulling me to my feet.

I dusted at the dirt left on my skin, seeing a few white scrapes along my legs, but nothing serious. "Thanks."

"Sure," he said, releasing his grip on my arm. Before I could push him away, he grabbed me and kissed me with a forceful intensity.

It only took a second for me to shove him off, taking a few steps back until I was on flat ground. "What the hell are you doing?"

"Sorry, I . . . " He chuckled as he wiped his arm across his mouth. "You looked too perfect."

My head jerked back, scoffing in sheer astonishment. "Wow. You really need to work on your pickup lines."

"You're not off limits, right? I mean, you were begging me to kiss you up there."

"Excuse me?" Shooting forward, I plucked my water bottle out of the side pocket of his bag. "I was gonna be nice about this, but screw that. Stay away from me."

I spun around and took off, hurrying as fast as my worn-out legs would go. The fucking nerve of him. I didn't once lead him on. Maybe before I was a bit of a flirt. God damn it, I really *was* Claire.

"Wait, don't storm off like that."

I felt his hand on my shoulder. With one swipe, I spun around, punching him square in the jaw. Pain shot through my knuckles into my wrist, but it was worth watching him fall back with his hand cradling his face. Eyes in complete, unexpected shock. "What the *hell*?"

"Don't touch me!" I leaned forward, narrowing my eyes. "You will *never* touch me again."

I was out of there, cutting down the path like the roadrunner cartoon. The fucking asshole. What an asshole! No wonder I ended up with guys like that.

A smile spread across my face when I reached the campground. My wrist was throbbing, but punching him was worth it.

It was what I should have done with Wes. I may not have had the balls to do it then, but I sure wasn't willing to experiment with that shit anymore.

"God damn it." I held my punching hand close to my chest, rubbing the skin to dissipate the pain. Despite my hand, I had never felt so proud of myself. I was practically flying over the manmade trail that entered the campground. Soaring past the trees and rocks like I was riding the wind. The bracelet around my wrist didn't harbor the weight of my past anymore. It was gone. Totally and completely gone.

I couldn't wait to tell Pete. To see him even. God, I hope he didn't hate me. I'd tell him everything. The mess I had been dealing with and how shitty I was for being afraid for so long. I'd tell him everything about Axel, how we were texting and how I wanted to mess around with him, if only to prove to myself that I didn't need him. But Axel helped me see where my fear was coming from and why I didn't need guys like him.

I hoped he'd forgive me. I'd kiss him a thousand times a day if he did. Never let go of his hand and nuzzle in the nook of his neck every night. I'd breathe in his watermelon scent or whatever bubble gum he chewed that day. We'd watch cheesy movies and just fucking live the way we wanted to without needing to impress anyone. It would be perfect. Special because we'd make it special together.

I noticed someone walking toward me who was just as frantic as me. When they got closer, they stopped. My eyes locked with his. "Pete."

He looked both relieved and completely lost. "Ash." He rushed over to me.

"I didn't mean to be gone so long."

He stopped just before reaching me, wiping his hand on his shorts. "I gotta tell you something."

"No, I have to tell you something." I licked my lips, keeping my hand close.

He peered down at my clenched fist. "What happened to your hand?"

"I punched that jerk in the face. He tried to kiss me and I decked his ass."

"You punched him?" His eyes drew away from me. "God, you're stronger than I am."

His voice sounded hopeless, jaded even. It sent a shockwave of prickling needles down my spine. "Pete." I grabbed his hands. They were clammy, maybe from nerves. His eyes spoke volumes, and I could sense that something was wrong as soon as I looked at him. "What . . . did you want to tell me?"

He looked down, biting his lip and shifting his feet. When he looked at me again, my heart sank.

"I kissed her," he said. "I kissed Kala."

twenty-seven

. . .

wyoming, thursday, august 13th

CLOSING my eyes was a death sentence. Every time I surrendered to the millisecond of darkness, I saw Pete and Kala. Kissing. Fucking kissing.

Fuck. Fuck. *Fuck.*

A deafening ringing in my ears had me madly dashing into our campsite. I wasn't functioning correctly. Tunnel vision took hold and all I could narrow in on was Kala, sitting on the picnic table with her head down on her knees.

She looked up with her face wet and hair plastered on her cheeks. I could hear Pete trying to get my attention, but my mind was on a mission. Getting the hell out of here.

"Kala." My voice was forward, but not harsh. "Get Gremlin and put him in the car."

Her legs hit the ground, confused at my request. "Ash—"

"*Get Gremlin.* Put him in the car," I practically shouted, with a sharp bite in my tone.

She scrambled from her seat and jogged over to the camper.

"What are you doing, Ash?" Pete's voice cut deeper than his confession.

With fists clenched, I turned around to Pete. "I'm leaving. Without you."

"To go where?"

"I don't give a *shit*! As long as it's away from you and this place!"

"God damn it, will you listen to yourself?" He ran his hands through his hair. "This is crazy."

"Fuck off, Pete!" As mad as I was, I still squeezed the hurt from my eyes. I didn't mean it. The logical side of me knew that, but I felt attacked. Like he was trying to hurt me, and maybe he was. I deserved it. I deserved all of it. But that doesn't make it hurt any less. It broke the chains of evil Ash when someone attacked me. "You know how hard it was? To say those things and push everything out of my head for you?"

"And do you know how hard it was for *me* to wait on the sidelines while you figured out your life?" My mouth shut tight as he stepped closer to me. "Every day is a battle with you. I . . . I don't know what to think anymore! What to feel. I go from high to the bottom of the fucking barrel within a day! It's exhausting and . . . this last thing just . . . "

Kala scurried over to the car with Gremlin inside his carrier. Opening the passenger door, she placed him inside before safely closing it. I heard her come up behind me, her words riddled with regret. "Ash, he didn't do anything wrong."

"Kala, don't lie for me." Pete sighed, his gaze shifting from me to her. He couldn't look at her straight, like he was afraid of what they would uncover if he did. Or maybe he didn't know what to feel. Meaning what to feel about me.

"Pete," Kala whispered. "No."

"I'm leaving." I turned and glared at Kala. "Stay with him, if you want."

Kala shook her head. "You can't leave . . . "

"Ash." Pete saying my name stung even harsher than before.

My fists clenched as I spun to face him again. *"Don't!"*

"Why? Why not?" His arms fell at his sides. "It's hard to hear the truth, huh? So, you're gonna run away like you aways do. You say you've changed, but you haven't. You're the same fucked-up girl I met on the street that day. *Exactly the same!*"

I pressed my teeth into my bottom lip so hard I tasted blood, letting the hurt leak through the gaps of my life. Maybe I hadn't changed, lying to make myself believe I could be someone different. Someone with a breakable heart. But I had left the wound to fester for too long; it was beyond repair.

My hands met his chest as I pushed him away. "And what are you?" My words caught in my throat as I pushed him again, gritting my teeth and squeezing my eyes. "You're a liar. *A fucking liar!*"

He didn't defend himself, letting me push him farther and farther away. "You're such a hypocrite! There's nothing left here! Nothing to hold on to. You've made it *impossible!*"

"So, this was just a colossal waste of time, then."

Every word deepened the cracks of this once hopeful relationship.

I grabbed his skateboard, backpack, and any other belongings from the seat and turned away so he wouldn't see me cry. "Take your shit!" I threw everything of his on the ground at his feet.

When I closed it again, my flight response went into overdrive. I couldn't look behind me. All I could do was open the driver's side and get in. I flipped the visor open and grabbed the keys. I put them in the ignition, drowning out the desperate attempts Pete was making for me to stop. His hands came down on the window.

"Get out, Ash. Get out of the car *now!*"

"No!" My head snapped as I pulled the parking break free. "This is *my* car. *My* camper. *My trip!* So *move!* Or I'll run you over."

His hands slammed against the car. "Ashley!"

Kala pulled Pete away, his head snapping to face him. "Stop!"

It felt like my cheeks were on fire, and my tears were like hot lava. Kala placed a gentle hand on the glass. "Ash. Open the window."

My finger trembled as it pressed the button, and the window slowly rolled open. Kala's face was so close to mine as she bent down to me, but I couldn't bring myself to look up. I knew she probably didn't mean to, but she hurt me. She said she wouldn't. She was a liar, just like Pete.

"Ash." I forced myself to look at her. She kept my gaze, not breathing a word, as the car rumbled in anticipation. I saw how sorry she was, the disappointment and pain I had created for her swimming in her unsteady eyes. The tip of my shoe traced the gas pedal, wanting to beat it out of there. I'd leave them both. I'd do it. But I also promised to bring her home. I couldn't leave her. I couldn't abandon her, even though she betrayed me.

Kala stood straight again, glancing to the left of the car before turning to Pete. "I'm going with Ashley."

Pete was taken aback. "What?"

"I'm sorry, Pete." She reached inside my window and pressed the button to unlock the car before rushing around the front. I was too shocked to stop her, even as the passenger side door opened and she sat down, buckling herself in.

"This is crazy." Pete reached for the door handle, but I locked it before he could pull it to open. "Ash. Get out of the car."

"No." I kept my eyes fixed ahead.

"Ash." He breathed. The faint smell of his summer taste wafted through the open window with every exhale. "Ashley!"

With a hard thrust, I sent the car into drive. Slamming my foot down on the gas and peeling out of the campsite. Pete threw himself back, barely avoiding the camper's edge as it zipped past him.

I left him in the dust. If I looked in the rearview mirror, I'd break into a thousand pieces. My head was on fire as we breached the park and pulled onto the main road. I could hear Kala crying softly to herself. It wasn't enough to pull me out.

In the midst of the downpour, I felt a sense of numbness wash over me as my eyes fragmented into a million raindrops.

I'm not sure how long we drove, but it was long enough that my sore muscles and throbbing head beat me into submission. We ended up pulling into a roadside motel where the occupancy was zero. The lady running the office was really kind. She saw us, two girls who were in a bad place, and gave us a room without needing to see my ID. Either she was taking pity on us or preparing to send in Norman Bates to kill us.

Rain pattered on the roof of the stretch along the walkway. Our room was quaint. Two double beds and a traditional nightstand in between. There was a rotary phone which was ancient. I never thought I'd come across one. Despite the dated décor, it smelled of tea tree oil and had complimentary snacks on the table. Not that I felt like eating. Dying would have been more appropriate.

Lying on the floral spread of one bed, I fell into my exhaustion. I couldn't think, let alone move. I felt like I got hit by a truck. And Pete. Fucking Pete. I left him alone in the middle of a national park.

What the hell is wrong with me?

"Ash."

Hearing Kala's soft voice was both infuriating and sad. I had every right to be mad at her, but didn't have the energy to confront her. I haphazardly pulled her between Pete and me as a last resort to escape the terror that was her father. She probably felt horrible. That was what made her so different from me. I wouldn't have given a shit.

"I don't really want to talk right now." My knees came up to my chest as I wrapped my arms around them. I just wanted to close my eyes and die. To be buried by a thousand pounds of dirt and call it a day. There was nothing I could do or say to justify what I had done. What I had forced Pete to do. Because I forced him. Shoving these two together with hot glue.

Kala settled on the other bed, and I could hear her sniffling to herself. Could I really let her stew in her guilt? I didn't even know if she felt guilty. Maybe that's why I didn't want to talk. Because I was afraid she'd say she was glad she kissed Pete. That she did it out of malice for my blatant stupidity.

Time went by in a flash as the moonlight rolled in the sky. I didn't know how long I had been awake. Despite how exhausted I was and how terrible I felt, I couldn't bring myself to fall asleep.

I couldn't fix it; there was no chance. So I told myself a beautiful lie. That Pete would forgive me. And repeated it in my head until my eyes closed and I was dead to all things.

When I finally recovered from my coma, the sun was glaring through the cracks of the dull peach curtains of the motel room. I leaned against my hand to push myself up, rubbing my eyes and scanning the room to get my bearings.

The sound of the running water stopped as Kala stepped out of the bathroom, her wet hair framing her face. When she saw me, she paused. "You're awake."

A wide yawn erupted from my mouth. "Yeah."

"Did you sleep okay?" Her words were genuine, with a slight layer of worry.

"As well as I could have, I guess."

We fell silent, waiting for the other to do something. Part of me still wanted to scream at her, but I felt like complete shit. At the very least, I needed to wash any evidence of yesterday from my body. I swung my stiff legs over the bed. "Let me shower. Then we'll find someplace to grab breakfast, okay?"

Tight-lipped, Kala nodded without a peep. I groaned as I stood up from the not-so-comfy bed. Shuffling over to the bathroom, I grabbed my comb and some other much needed amenities from my backpack, which sat on one chair. My phone was there too. Cautiously, I picked it up and checked if I had any messages.

None.

"Have you heard from Pete?" I asked without bothering to look at her.

I could hear the tenseness of her breath as she exhaled. "He texted me," Kala spoke softly. "He got a ride."

He texted *her*. Just another sign that he hated my guts. I didn't think it was necessary to reply, so I headed to the bathroom. Any relief the news of him gave me drained from my face as quickly as the water pattered against the cheap shower tile. I focused on the drops as they pelted my skin, relieving me of my sore muscles and equally sore heart.

twenty-eight

...

wyoming, friday, august 14th

WE PILED in the car after checking on Gremlin and giving him his breakfast. There was a small diner not too far from the motel and we pulled in to get some much needed energy back into our bodies. I sat across from Kala, who barely looked at me. She studied the menu like it was a final exam.

I wondered how they kissed. If it was just a quick peck, or did he hold her like he held me? Did he take her face in his hands and suck in the scent of her as he tasted her lips? Did Pete kiss her, or did Kala kiss him? I knew what they said, but I didn't know what the truth was. More lies on top of lies. I was so tired of lies.

Crossing my arms on the table, I peered out of the window as the waitress dropped off my coffee and Kala's orange juice on the table. "Hey."

Kala looked up, pushing her curtain of hair away from her eyes.

"You okay?"

Those two brief words trembled her lip and shielded her eyes. "No." Her hand came up to wipe at her premature tears.

I held my tongue back from committing any lashes. I wanted this to be a civil conversation. This was an emotional rollercoaster for everyone involved, not just me. And Kala didn't stay with Pete. That had to mean something.

"You were right." She came up for air. "I am falling for Pete. And . . . he didn't kiss me. I kissed him."

The back of my throat closed. *Fuck.* I thought I would feel different hearing the truth, but it didn't matter anymore. Pete still said all those terrible things to me. He texted Kala over me. He went with the lie that *he* kissed Kala. I remained silent to let everything she had said, and was about to say, soak into my skin.

"He was so upset after he came back from your hike together. I let him be, but . . . I was worried about him. So, we talked and I just . . . I couldn't help myself."

I leaned back against the plastic cushion of the booth, dropping my clenched hands into my lap. "He didn't stop you."

"No." She shook her head. "He didn't. Not at first." My attention returned to her. Kala laid her hands on the table, her fingers fidgeting at its surface. "He wanted to tell you right away, and I told him not to. He said it was wrong not to tell you."

"Why did you not want to tell me?"

"Because." Her chin dropped for a second before she looked up at the ceiling as she tried to compose herself. "It scared me that you would hate me because I lied to you . . . about what I was feeling. And that you wouldn't want to be my friend anymore." She let out a breathless sigh as her water-drenched eyes fell on me. "I know that sounds childish."

"Is that why you came with me?" I asked.

Kala's fingers curled into her palms against the table. "I knew I'd hurt you. And I didn't want you to be alone. I wanted to be there for you, like you were for me. Even if you never wanted to be friends afterward."

I closed my eyes, building up the sticks and twigs to keep myself from cracking. "I'm sorry."

"Sorry? For what?"

I came back to her as she moved her hands off the table.

"Everything. Acting like I have been. Dragging you into my shit." I breathed a sigh as I dropped my arms back on the table. "I left him there. What the hell is wrong with me?"

"He's okay."

"No." My face buried in my arms, letting a few drops fall to relieve the pressure building up behind my eyes. I should have been the bigger person. Like a stampede of wild buffalo, I reacted instead of thinking. I didn't have to bail on him. Maybe I could have found some place to cool off and come back with a level head to work it out. But I ran away to avoid dealing with the problem. Just like I'd always done. I wiped my face against my arm before sitting up again. "I screwed up big time."

Silence passed between us as the confession settled into the booth. Now I was having a hard time looking at Kala, knowing that I couldn't apologize enough for all the bullshit I had dragged her into. And Pete. He may have found a ride, but a ride to where? Was he going to the airport? Fed up enough to leave for home and never come back?

My heart hit the floor. I wanted to see him again. Apologize for leaving and get closure. But I also wanted to beg him to forgive me. Because I couldn't bear the thought of losing him. Even if he kissed a hundred girls. This was something I couldn't do over the phone. That was what the old me would do. I had to see him. Face to face.

"If I scared you, I apologize for that, too." I gave a weak smile. "You got a dose of the New York Ashley out there."

"I wasn't scared." Kala slipped the straw of her OJ between her lips and took a sip. "I'm so sorry, Ashley. I really am."

"I know. You don't have to apologize to me." I shrugged. "Thanks for saying it, though."

Another few minutes of silence ticked by. The waitress brought us our food. Scrambled eggs, sausage, and hash browns for me. And a bowl of oatmeal with a fruit cup for Kala. I stared at the massacred eggs like they were the projection of my brain. If I ate them, would I feel more in control of my life?

"So, what now?" Kala asked.

I gave her a weak smile to make things less uncomfortable. "I'm gonna take you home like I promised."

"Okay."

We ate the rest of our breakfast in silence, pointing out things here and there, but mostly kept our words simple. The last few days of this journey would be like an inevitable ending to a tragic tale. *No Fear Shakespeare* in living color.

twenty-nine

· · ·

WE HAD 12 hours of driving ahead of us. During that 12 hours, Pete hadn't called or texted. Axel did. Multiple times. But screw him.

I didn't contact Pete. If I tried, my fingers would just hover over the keypad, mulling over words that weren't meaningful enough to translate how I felt. He had said some pretty nasty things and if he believed any of them, then getting a text from me would be laughable.

Kala was a fucking angel. Never brought up Pete once, never asked to talk about everything that happened. She made me glad I wasn't alone. She distracted me with stories of her life, how choosing to live with her dad was the hardest decision she ever had to make. About losing their home because he couldn't hold a job and it forced them to live out of an RV. But it wasn't all sob stories.

She talked about her mom, and how she made a mean *huevos a la mexicana*. Most of our conversations were about food, honestly. I could tell she was really passionate about it.

"I've never even heard of *huevos a la mexicana*," I told her.

"It has tomatoes and chili peppers. Eggs with cilantro that you fry with onions in a skillet." The thought brought a satisfying smile to her face. "*Perfecto.*"

I laughed at her enthusiasm. "I bet that's the first thing you ask for when you get home."

"I'll have to make it for you one day. Do you cook?"

I shook my head. "Only basic stuff. I can handle spaghetti, okay?"

She shook her head. "That's not actual food."

"Tell that to any Italian in New York and they'll put a hit out on you."

It became a girls' trip. And it was like I'd known Kala for years instead of weeks. But once we laid down in the camper or motel, depending on what we could find on this derailed road, I couldn't close my eyes without seeing Pete's face. Without hearing his voice and reliving the words he said to me. And the last kiss before it all came crashing down.

We dropped the camper off at the rental place before driving through the streets of LA to her house. The structure of the city was the same, but it had a different feel than New York. New York always felt heavy, like a film of dirt was constantly surrounding it. But maybe that was because so much awful shit happened there. So many things I would rather forget. California was new and untainted.

"This is me." Kala pointed out the window.

We pulled up to a small house that was identical to all the rest. It was peach colored. A cement walkway cut through a small patch of grass to get to the dark green door, flanked on both sides by squared windows. I shifted the car into park.

"You should come in." Kala's request singed my nerves.

"No, it's okay."

"Come on." She pulled at my arm. "My mom will come out here anyway and insist."

The seat belt came off as I dragged myself from the car. Following her up the walkway, I couldn't quite place the nerves. Kala hooked her arm with mine, giving me a look that said it all.

"I don't know why I'm so nervous," she said. "I haven't seen my mom in a year."

"I'm nervous for you. But you'll be okay."

"I know, 'cause you're here with me." She smiled as we came to the door.

Her words shocked me awake. Why did she need me? I dragged her into a proverbial mess of a situation and she wasn't the least bit put-off by it.

Before her finger touched the doorbell, it swung open to a short, shapely woman with rough sanded skin and a sweet smile. Kala suddenly stopped and grinned ear-to-ear. She let go of my arm and hugged her mom.

"*Mi pajarito!*" Her mother was already in tears as she stroked Kala's hair and squeezed her tight, a reflection of all the missed hugs over the last year they were apart.

"*Re extrañé, mamá.*" Kala sniffed loudly, absorbing all the love robbed from her for too long.

I wasn't fluent in Spanish, but I knew they said they missed each other, and it filled me with an overwhelming sense of joy. It came full circle, seeing them together; why Kala was with her alcoholic father over her mother. It reminded me of how I had been with Wes. She wanted to save her father, even though he never asked to be saved.

When they finally pulled apart, her mother looked her over like she had just come in from a day of playing in the mud.

"You are radiant, Zitkala. *Tan hermosa!*" Her mothering eyes cast to me. "And who is this?"

Kala looked at me with the warmest sense of assuredness. "This is the girl who saved me. Ashley." The next few seconds passed in silence. Kala's demeanor reverted to that unsure girl I found sitting at the picnic table in the Badlands. "We're still friends, right?"

I couldn't move, let alone speak. I didn't know if it was the warm, fuzzy feeling in the air or if this question of friendship kicked up an unexpected moment of clarity. Despite everything that had happened and everything that might come because of it, I realized what a kindred spirit Kala had become. She was *so much* like me. A younger version of me that, if someone knocked some sense into me sooner, I'd surely be more like.

"Of course we're friends."

My eyes choked up as her mother held out her arms to me with a warm embrace. "Thank you. Thank you for bringing *mi pajarito* home."

Her mother smelled of sweet peppers. When she let me go, the smile on her face made my heart swell. "Come. Come inside."

"No. I can't. Really. I need to go."

"Then you come back soon. I will cook for you. Kala's friends are always welcome here."

She stepped away, and Kala replaced her. She practically lunged into my arms; I barely caught her. I couldn't contain my happiness as I felt her gratitude wash over me, and a few tears escaped down my cheeks.

"Thank you for everything," she whispered in my ear.

My face nestled in her coal-streaked hair. I had done what I said I would do. I saved her. And as messed up as the entire rescue mission was, she was grateful. And so was I.

thirty

. . .

california, monday, august 17th

"YO, ASH. WHERE YOU AT?" Dimitri rattled off without skipping a beat.

Parked in the street outside Kala's house, I closed the door to the car, shifting the phone in my hand. "I'm in California."

"You in LA?"

"Yeah. Just had to drop off the camper. I'll be there soon."

"All right, hurry. Don't make any stops."

My brow furrowed at his immediate need for me to get to his apartment. "Why can't I make any stops?"

"Just . . . get here, okay?"

I didn't want to press it, so I'd listen. "Okay."

A faint lip smack came through the receiving speaker. "See you soon."

It seemed odd he didn't ask me about anything else. Not about Pete especially. I'd only texted him once Kala and I left Utah, saying I was on my way to California. Maybe Max was giving him grief about something.

I popped on some Six Leaves Left to keep myself calm for the ride.

I couldn't stop twitching my fingers on the wheel or bouncing my leg against the floor of the Subaru. How was I going to explain showing up alone?

Pulling up to the apartment building, I turned the corner to the parking lot. Each apartment had a designated spot, but neither Dimitri nor Max owned a car, so I was in the clear. I found 203 and settled my car between the lines, killing the engine. It was quiet, with only the sounds of the street to keep me occupied.

My gaze traveled to my hands, tossing and turning in my lap like I lost them in a restless sleep. My fingers clutched my bracelet as I lay back against the headrest. "Dad." I closed my eyes, so I could imagine standing in front of him, his expression never changing. "I'm sorry I tried to forget you."

He moved this time, finding me as he bent down for us to meet on level ground. *"You have nothing to be sorry for, ladybug."* His hands pressed to my shoulders, spreading my unsteady lips across my face. *"Just take a second."* A gentle pressure was all I needed to wake myself up.

Breathe in.

Breathe out.

Turning in my seat, I looked at Gremlin in the carrier. His fat, furry face purred through the mesh. Yellow eyes squinting in satisfaction as he gave me a gentle meow.

"You ready for this, Gremlin?" I asked as my chin leaned against the headrest. "I hope I am."

Grabbing the essential stuff first, I threw my bag over my shoulder before slipping Gremlin's carrier into my hand. I'd have to come back and get the rest of the gear. There was still a lot of shit in the car, some of it Pete's. Whenever I got around to talking to him again, I'd have to send it to him. Wherever he was.

I rang the bell for 203.

"Yo," Dimitris' voice crackled through the intercom.

"Hey. It's me."

The door buzzed, and I pushed it open. The lobby was wide with mailboxes along both stretches of wall before narrowing into the first floor hallway. I opted to take one flight of stairs, because the more I moved, the less anxious I felt.

The second floor landing had a few benches and a table with magazines thrown on top. As I stepped off the stairs, I noticed a body slouched on the bench.

When they saw me, they sat up. Bleach blond hair wafted from his crown. Red Hawaiian beach shorts matched well with his orange surfer tank, skin tan from the California sun, and a pair of flip-flops on his feet.

It took me a second to figure him out, but when I did, I almost dropped Gremlin's carrier on the floor. "Logan."

"Hey, Carter." He waved lazily. "You're here."

"Yeah." I walked cautiously toward Pete's best friend from Hicksville High, stopping at the table. "And so are you." I scrunched my eyebrows, looking toward the hallway just beyond. "Why are you?"

I knew why Logan was in California for his skateboarding thing, but why he was here, in my brother's apartment building, waiting for me . . .

"Well, that's an interesting story." He rubbed his hands together between his knees.

My heart jumped into my throat. "Pete's . . . here."

"Yeah. He's here."

With careful concentration, I lowered Gremlin's carrier to the floor. "Holy shit." I drunkenly made it to the bench, slinging my bag from my shoulder as I flopped down next to him. "Shit. Shit. Shit."

My hands pressed against my temples as I attempted to pop my brain out of my skull. My forehead was pounding so hard that I couldn't hear anything, and my legs were too jittery to relax.

"You okay?"

"Do I look okay?" My eyes snapped to him. "No. I'm not fucking okay." I couldn't slow down my breathing and my heart felt like it was about to burst out of my chest, classic *Alien* style. "What am I gonna say?"

Logan exhaled sharply through his teeth. "I don't know, Carter. This is a pretty screwed up situation."

I closed my eyes, trying to remember how to breathe.

In and out. In and out.

I broke away from my hands, leaning my head against the wall. "This is all my fault." Logan stayed quiet, his thumb rubbing against the other in his folded hands. "You picked him up?"

He nodded. "Yeah. Got him in Utah and we made the trek back."

"How long since you've been back?"

"Pulled in yesterday. He crashed at my place before coming here." Logan peered at me. "Listen, I don't know everything," his hands motioned toward me, "that's going on here. With you and him. But I've never seen him so messed up over anything."

My head came off the wall. I wasn't about to get into it with Pete's best friend. Not knowing what he already told him, and vice versa. It wasn't my business. But part of me was relieved Pete was here. A chance at redemption, or maybe a chance to fix this.

"Thanks for picking him up, Logan." I put my hand on his arm. "Seriously. You're a good friend."

He took a quick peek at our contact. "Okay, who are you and what have you done with Ashley Carter?"

That crack forced a smile to my lips. "Funny." I drew my hand away and looked toward the stairs. "I guess I better get in there, then."

"You'll be all right." Logan nodded as I turned to him. "No matter what, it'll work out how it should."

"Are you always so positive?"

He shrugged. "Someone's gotta be, right?"

I smirked again. "Thanks, Logan."

I dragged myself onto my feet and gathered my things for the anxiety-ridden journey down the hall to apartment 203. Every step was another deep breath in and a long one out. I kept my eyes to the floor, still unable to hear anything but the relentless pulse sounding in my ears. When I got to the door, I stopped and so did my heart. I wasn't sure if I could knock, but luckily I didn't have to.

Max opened the door with Dimitri right behind her. Her hair was curly and magnificent as ever, with her model curves wrapped up in a cute polka dot romper.

"Ash." She wrapped me in a deep hug as I desperately absorbed all manner of strength from it as I could.

"Hey, Max," I whispered.

"Damn it, Ash." Dimitri's dark face and shaved head shook as he stepped through the door frame. "The shit you pull."

Max drew away from me and gave him a sharp look. "Tri, not helping right now."

"All right." His arm came out to me, pulling me into his broad, stocky chest. "Glad you made it in one piece, Sis."

"Good to see you, too." It felt good to be in his arms. Not only because he was a linebacker with the bulk to show for it, but because he was my brother, a taste of home. Of a life I often wished I could still be in. I didn't want him to let go because that meant I would have to walk through the door and face the biggest mess of my life. But I couldn't run, even if I tried. Dimitri wouldn't let me. And I wouldn't let myself either.

When he finally drew away, he looked down at my worry-stricken face. "You nervous?"

"Nervous isn't a big enough word."

"You should be." He sighed. "But I'm proud of you."

"Doesn't mean I don't want to run."

"You can want to. But you're not." He smirked, his fist coming up to nudge my chin like he used to do when we were kids.

"He's in the front room." Max put her hand on the strap covering my shoulder. I glanced at her. "Go in. If you're ready."

My bag slowly fell into her hand. I gingerly handed her Gremlin's carrier, biting my tongue as I stepped into the apartment.

"Is the car open?" Dimitri asked. "I'll get the rest of your stuff."

"Yeah," I said, handing him the keys. "Thanks."

Max dropped my bag and Gremlin into the kitchen and followed Dimitri out. "We'll be right back, okay?"

The door shut behind them, and I was alone. Alone with my greatest regret.

The front room was literally around the corner from their boho and sports decorated apartment. Hangings of feathers and rope adorned the walls right beside football trophies and an open, sweaty gym bag. I took off my purple Converse and put them next to the rack, walking barefoot across the thin runner.

I placed my hands on the wall, pressing my forehead against it with my eyes closed.

I've got this.

I wasn't sure what was about to happen. Would I collapse into tears at the sight of him? Or scream my head off to make myself feel like I was bigger than he was? I vaguely imagined a fish out of water, desperately trying to flip itself into a puddle that was an inch away. But instead of floundering uncontrollably like I normally would be, I had control now. I always had. I just wasn't brave enough to take the wheel until now.

I peeked around the corner and there he was. His back to me, elbows leaning on his knees, and slouched forward. His hair was messier than usual against the vintage batman tee he wore.

"Hey." The sound of my voice spun him around like a top.

"Hi." His voice was strained, revealing the hurt he was feeling. I wanted to burst out crying, but I stayed collected.

I slid into the room. Pete's eyes followed me as I took a seat in the armchair across from him. I settled into the cushions, half wishing they would swallow me up. "I didn't think I'd see you again."

"Yeah." He sighed. "I didn't think so either."

"I saw Logan. He said he picked you up in Utah."

He nodded slowly. "Yeah. Axel and his gang gave me a ride. Believe it or not."

I leaned to the right. "Really?"

"Yeah." He sat up a bit. "After you beat it, he came looking for you. Wanted to apologize. Found me instead and said I could hitch a ride with them if I needed to get somewhere."

"Wow. That was . . . nice of him."

His lips tightened. "Did Kala make it home okay?"

I rolled my tongue across my teeth, putting a gentle pressure on them as my gaze fell to the multi-striped rug. "Yeah. I just came from dropping her off."

"Good." He paused. "She . . . was she okay? After everything?"

My head came up with a nod, but I couldn't say anything in reply. He cared about Kala more than me, otherwise he wouldn't have asked about her. Not first. Not in this moment. Nothing might be okay again, but I had to try. "Did—" I choked down my words, keeping them locked inside my lungs.

"Stop." Pete shook his head. "Please stop talking."

Our eyes locked, both so full of regret neither one of us blinked. His hands slid up his legs. "I'm sorry. I said . . . horrible things to you. I . . . I don't think that. I don't think that about you."

A question lingered on the tip of my tongue that would shatter me if I knew the answer. But if I didn't ask him, it would never let me rest soundly again. "Did you want to kiss Kala?"

His mouth tightened, fists clenched against his shorts. "I don't know. In the moment, yes. I wanted to. Now, I don't know."

My face dropped, along with a few tears for the truth that drenched my skin. "Okay."

"It's not okay."

I wiped the sadness from my cheeks before meeting his eyes again.

"I don't want you to hurt. But I don't want to hurt, either."

"I know. And I've hurt you. I left you and . . . I've been . . . terrible and I'm . . . so, so sorry for treating you so terribly." My eyes clenched. "And . . . you can hate me." My chin quivered. "And that'll be fine."

"Damn it, Ash." Pete pushed off the couch and came to kneel before me, grabbing my hands to shake me into consciousness. "I can't hate you. Trust me, I've tried."

That last comment pulled a momentary smirk out of the dark, matched by one of his own. It quickly depleted, because I knew what I had to do if we were ever going to heal. I gripped his hands and wished we could just forget it all. But I couldn't leave a wound open and hope it would get better. It would only fester, and eventually, I'd have to cut it out.

I bit my lip, trying to suppress my emotions and prevent myself from speaking. I let my mouth open to silence before allowing the words I never wished to say to spill out. "Maybe we need a break . . . for a while. Just . . . let ourselves be."

He nodded, his mouth tight as his eyes closed. "Yeah." He turned his head slightly, so he wasn't facing me. "I think that's a good idea."

"You're important to me." I pulled his hands closer, forcing his gaze on me again. "I don't think you know . . . just how important you are."

A sudden twitch caused his brow to crash against his eyes. "Maybe one day I will."

I took a deep breath, keeping our hands intertwined in my lap. "Are you heading back, then? To New York?"

"No. Logan said I could crash with him. I'll . . . I'll stay here."

I couldn't stop my heart from fluttering. The hope that was slowly burning out pulsed to life again.

He was staying.

Pete cast his gaze to our joined hands. "I guess . . . I guess I should go."

His fingers loosened around mine, but I wasn't ready to let him leave. With one fell swoop, I threw my arms around his neck, burrowing into my most favorite place in the world. He didn't push me away; he held me close, breathing in the scent of my hair as our hearts beat in perfect rhythm for the other.

"Thank you," I whispered through my longing. "For saving me."

I felt him slip away, but his hands settled on my face and kept my gaze on his. I was fighting myself, from kissing him, from wanting to beg him to stay. But despite all the apologies and regret, it buried us under too much to breathe without choking. I still didn't know how bad the damage was or how he felt about Kala. I didn't think he knew either.

His forehead rested against mine, rendering me sightless as I closed my eyes and just relished in the feel of his hands on my face.

His harsh breath seeped into my skin. I grasped his wrists and committed this moment to memory, keeping his watermelon scent locked away for all the days I would be without him.

It took every ounce of control I had to let him go. Our eyes met one last time before my hands fell from his arms. Upon standing, I watched him walk toward the kitchen. When he disappeared behind the wall, and I heard the door open and close, I let myself slide from the chair onto the floor.

I'm not sure how long I just sat there, staring at nothing, locked in wavering uncertainty. It wasn't until Max came in, kneeling beside me to take me in her arms, that I allowed myself to let the pieces fall.

thirty-one
. . .

california, tuesday september 2nd

THE DAYS WERE all dragged into one. A minute became hours of me staring out the window as the clouds passed and the sun rose and set over the many tall buildings of Los Angeles. With my legs curled against my chest, I rested my chin down on my knees. Iron and Wine pumped into my ears, filling and emptying me all at the same time. I'd been this way for days, weeks. I couldn't tell the difference.

I barely ate. Barely moved. I couldn't sleep without seeing Pete's face each time I closed my eyes. We didn't talk once. Not a single text or emoji passed between us since he had left. Amber called me a hundred times and I couldn't get through a single sentence without crying my eyes out. I didn't know how to function without him here. It was like everything shut off the second I uttered those words.

Maybe we need a break for a while.

I condemned us both. But it wasn't because I wanted us to fail. I wanted us to be better. To come back and prove that this love was real. And here I was. Messing it all up. I hadn't been able to collect myself from the crash. All the pieces left scattered across the floor. I thought maybe a day or two of this and I could start again. But it was impossible.

Gremlin rubbed his furry self across my back, momentarily pulling me back to the couch and out of the clouds. Turning around, I scooped him up and placed him in my lap. He immediately stretched his forelegs up against mine and closed his eyes with a gentle purr. Why Pete didn't take him, I didn't know. But if this was the only thing of himself he left with me, I would never let him go.

"Yo." Dimitri popped his head from around the corner. "Gotta minute?"

I quietly nodded, taking off my headphones. He came over and sat down on the coffee table to be next to me. "What are you doing, Ash?"

I couldn't even fathom a response, letting my shoulders respond for me as they came up and back down again.

Dimitri sighed, glancing out the window of my life for the past two weeks. "You gonna sit here and sulk, for the rest of you life? That's your plan?"

"I don't know what else to do." I looked down at Gremlin, dragging my fingers across the top of his black and brown head.

"How 'bout gettin' up and doing something?" Dimitri sat up. "You decided this and now you gotta own it."

"D, I have no clue what I'm doing anymore." I closed my eyes. "I'm so scared to take a step without him."

"Hey." His hand touched my arm, forcing me to focus. "What'd I tell you before? I got your back. Through all of this. So stand up. Hold your breath. And push yourself forward." He huffed. "You think Pete's gonna wanna see you like this, weeks or months from now?"

"No." I gave a half-hearted shrug.

"All you need is your own two feet. Do it for yourself. 'Cause you got you all the time. Make a better you."

The corner of my mouth twitched, a smirk quickly dragging across my face. "How?"

His flexed biceps came around me and squeezed. It didn't matter how many times he hugged me, it always felt like the first time. I feared the world around me, but I knew the second those arms held me and pulled me in, nothing could hurt me.

"I love you, Ashley." He planted a kiss on my cheek before pulling away. "Now get in the kitchen and tell Max to drag your ass out."

Dimitri grabbed Gremlin and pulled him off my lap before grabbing my wrist and hauling me up. I didn't object, but standing on my own two feet was a little uneasy after all the wallowing I'd been doing.

"Okay." I huffed, fixing the sleeves of my tee like Max would give a shit how I looked. I followed him into the kitchen, Gremlin hanging from his arm like a rag doll. Max was fixing up something delicious, or at least it smelled delicious. Sporting a short floral dress that highlighted her long legs, she had her hair tied back in a neat bun.

"Yo, Max." Dimitri came beside her, leaning against the counter.

"Yeah?" She turned and noticed me standing by the table. "You're up."

I nodded. "Yeah. For good, I hope."

"Oh, yeah?" She turned and crossed her arms, wooden spoon in hand. "So, what's your plan?"

I hesitated, looking from Dimitri to Max. They both watched me with hopeful gleams in their eyes as the food sizzled and sparked on the stovetop. I took a deep breath. "Get a job. Maybe go to school."

"Okay." Max pulled a brochure off the counter and walked over to me, shoving it into my hands.

I looked it over, seeing the word 'cosmetology' strewn across the front. "Cosmetology school?"

"It's where I teach and got my license. 18 months of hair. It's no walk in the park, competitive as hell, but I think you've got the attitude for it." I looked up at Max. She had a brow raised and a half smirk decorating her face. "What do you say?"

I didn't know exactly what I was committing to. I wasn't huge about hair, even though I had a lot of it. But it was an opportunity to change. And who knows, maybe I'd be good at it. I would try anything if it meant I wasn't thinking about the *what ifs*. I had to be present in the *moment*.

I nodded as I leaned to the left. "Let's go for it."

Max gave me a massive hug, grinning from ear to ear. I'd do it. And I'd pour all my impulses and irrational thinking into doing it right.

thirty-two

· · ·

california, wednesday, january 11th

"CARAMEL MACCHIATO FOR KANEDA!" I slid the brewed drink across the counter as a tall, lean, muscled guy with dark hair and deep hooded eyes came up to grab it. He was a regular here lately, young, probably close to my age, wearing boxing shorts and a dark tank. He looked tough, but not Wes tough, more like *Rurouni Kenshin* tough, minus the scar on the face.

"Thanks," he said with a grin.

I adjusted the straps of my Starbucks apron and gave him a teasing smirk. "So, are you a professional boxer or something?"

"What gave you that idea?" He raised his drink.

I looked him up and down. "You look like you just got out of a ring."

He gave a wicked, charming smile. "I take Muay Thai. Kickboxing."

"Well, Kaneda the kickboxer," his smile drew me in, "I hope you enjoy your coffee."

"I'm sure I will. I always want you to handle my caffeine when you're here."

I leaned against the counter, raising a brow. "That all I'm good for? Making coffee?"

"Well," he gave a single shrug, "I don't know you well enough yet."

I raised my eyebrow. "Yet?"

Despite toning down my flirtatious nature recently, I couldn't resist the urge when this guy came around. He was hot as hell.

Kaneda breathed a nervous scoff. "Actually, I—"

"Ashley!" I turned to find my boss waving a few cups in my general direction. "Orders!"

I came back to Kaneda with a grin. "Sorry, gotta get back to it. Have an enjoyable night."

I didn't stick around to hear a reply. Making my way toward Angel, my boss, I ripped the cups from his hands as he watched me with his pudgy face and patchy facial hair. "Where's Kala? She's late."

I shrugged. "I don't know. Probably off with that new guy of hers."

"Well, she better get here soon. I can't afford to pay you overtime."

I backed away to the brewer. "As much as I would love to rob this place of more dough, I have a class in an hour, so I am right there with you on that."

I threw the cups on the counter to start the coffee making process. It'd been a rough four months, but I felt like I finally had control of my life. I had fourteen more to go to get my cosmetology license, but I liked it. It made me want to work harder. Do better.

Axel had come out of the shadows again. He had apologized and was back in California now. He had asked me a hundred times if I wanted to hang out, but I couldn't bring myself to do it. If I could avoid people like him in my life, I would. I was grateful that he helped Pete, and I thanked him for that, but there was nothing there. Not as a lover. Not as a friend.

And Pete, we were communicating again, sparingly. After about a month or so, he hit me up. Just a random text or a silly meme that only we would get. We never asked questions, never popped in a, "So, when can I see you?" I got the feeling he wasn't ready for that, so I would continue to wait until he was. Honestly, I was just happy he didn't erase me.

Kala was a constant in my life now. We hung out all the time. I even got her a job here at Starbucks. She was finishing up her senior year, and I couldn't be more proud of her. The girl we picked up in South Dakota was an entirely new person. She even had a boyfriend now, though I haven't met him yet. This was her first, so I totally get her being weird about it.

"Hey, sorry I'm late!" Kala rushed in, slipping out of her black and pink hoodie before disappearing to the back.

I finished up the order I was working on, delivered it to the counter, and untied my apron. Slipping through the backdoor, I hung it on my hook as I watched Kala scramble to get hers on.

"I'm so sorry! I lost track of time," she said as she tied her hair up.

"It's okay. You know I'll cover you."

"Yeah, but you have class. I just spaced."

I smirked. "Hanging out with your guy, I take it?"

Her eyes flashed in embarrassment as she turned away to close her locker.

"When am I gonna meet him, anyway?"

"He's just . . . he's shy."

Pulling open my locker, I grabbed my messenger bag and closed it. "I think you're just too nervous to share your secret boy toy."

"He's not my boy toy."

I nudged her. "Relax, Kala. Seriously. Whenever you're ready to introduce me to him, I'm here for it."

I slung my bag over my shoulder, making for the door.

"Ash—"

"Sorry, Kala. I gotta get to class." I waved playfully at her. "Enjoy Angel's attitude for the night!"

I shifted through the nightly rush of caffeine addicted customers toward the exit. Opening the door to the outside world, the sights and sounds of LA filtered through my ears. It always smelled like summer in the city. The ocean air carried a sense of newness that differed from New York. I missed little things about Long Island, but there was so much I'd left behind. Things I wouldn't rush to get back to anytime soon.

Rummaging through my bag for my headphones, I turned to the right to make my way to class.

"Hey there."

I froze, my headphones dropping back into my bag. Pete stood, leaning against the full-paned windows of Starbucks. He had on a plain black tee with blue jeans, earbuds wrapped around his neck. His hair was longer, finger brushed back with pomade to the right. His glasses were just like I remembered them, framing his smiling brown eyes. God, he looked fucking amazing. Even better than I remembered.

My heart stopped, sending a massive attack of butterflies to my stomach. "Hi," I squeezed out of my breathless lungs. It's been over four months since he left my brother's apartment. "What are you doing here?"

He nudged toward the window. "Just walking Kala to work."

I could feel the blade of the knife waver before it finally plunged into my heart, and I squeezed my eyes shut in anticipation. Part of me hoped he loved me enough to wait, even if it took twenty years. But that was selfish. I did too much damage and realized too late. The singing in my ears turned to sorrowful moans of regret as I tried to rid his words from my mind. But it permanently stained them on impact.

"Oh," I managed, as I forced myself to look at him. "So, you're *the* guy."

He hesitated. "Yeah." His hand moved to the back of his neck. "I thought Kala would've told you by now."

"You know her." I tried to shrug it off playfully but failed to hide my plea. "She probably thought I'd flip."

We stood awkwardly, letting people with important things to do or nothing at all move past us like blurred lines on wet paper. I wanted to run back into work, pull Kala from behind the counter, and scream in her face. How could she not tell me? My best friend . . .

"Where are you headed?" he asked.

I came back to him, letting the growing weight of my legs keep me planted. "I have class. Cosmetology school."

"Yeah, Kala told me you've been doing that." He took a step away from the window. "Can I walk you there?"

The urge to run into an alley and ball my brains out was overbearing. But there was still so much left to unpack. So many wrongs that no one should forgive me for. I couldn't run away. I would not play that game again.

"Sure." I came up beside him and we made our way down the lighted streets and bustling traffic. My hands fell to my sides beside his, which sat comfortably in his pockets. Every so often, he would come close enough that I brushed against his arm. I wanted to hold on to him, to feel his hand in mine and have him say he was just kidding. Even though it was Kala. Even though we both decided that being apart was the best thing for us. I didn't want to believe that he would not choose me. Despite it only being a chance.

"So," I kept my eyes on the sidewalk, "how long have you and Kala been going out?"

"Just since her birthday. So . . . maybe a month?" He shrugged. "I know she's only a year younger, but the under eighteen thing kind of made me nervous."

"Now she's fair game?" He looked at me with that infectious grin of his, and I immediately regretted my words. "Sorry. I didn't mean to play it off like that—"

"Nah, don't worry."

My gaze returned to the sidewalk. "So, I guess you're sticking around LA for a while, then?"

We came to a corner. I stayed close to him, absorbing the brush of his arm like water on a dying flower. When we made it to the other side, we continued our walk at a safe distance. "Yeah, for a long while. Got into UCLA. Start next week."

"Wow, Pete, that's . . . awesome." It *was* awesome, but showing it was something I couldn't convey right now.

His eyes came to me. "Dimitri talked me into it."

"Dimitri? My brother, Dimitri?"

"Yeah. I went on campus to check it out and ran into him. He gave me the complete tour, and we kinda got into it."

A shot of anger stung the blood rushing through my veins at the fact that Dimitri never told me about this. But I didn't let that cloud the reality. Dimitri was present for all the aftermath. Just the mention of Pete would trip me up. He was probably trying to protect me. "You gonna dorm there?"

"No. I'm sticking with Logan for as long as I can. It's cheaper staying at his apartment. His school pays for it."

Another smirk crossed my face. "How has living with Logan been? Interesting?"

"It's been . . . unusual."

We both leaked out a snicker. "I'm happy for you, Pete. Seriously."

"Thanks." We crossed another street, Pete brushing against me again before we made it to the other side. "So, I know about your cosmetology school. Kala says you're liking it, okay?"

"Yeah, it clicks. I'll be licensed in another year."

"When you are, I'll be your first customer."

I refrained from speaking, as I was at a loss for words.

Pete glanced at me. It looked like he wasn't ready to stop talking. "Anything else going on? How's Gremlin?"

"He's lazy. Definitely put on a few pounds since coming here."

"I miss that fuzzball. I'm glad I left him with you, though."

"Why?"

He shrugged. "You needed him."

My blood was practically forming icicles along my arms. Pete's gaze fell to the sidewalk for a split second. "Seeing anyone?"

I shook my head, the acknowledgement of my hopelessness daunting to hear. "No. No. Just work and class."

"That's not necessarily bad, right?"

I didn't answer and just kept counting the cracks on the sidewalk as we headed toward my school. The rest of the walk was silent, my mind battling with how I was going to get any words out.

When we finally got to the building, I stopped in the streetlight's buzz. "This is me."

Pete was a few steps ahead before stopping in front of it. "Cool."

I stepped toward him, afraid of the terrible memories I was about to dig up. It was a harsh reality that he had moved on and I was stuck in this illusion of us. It was stupid to think I was impervious, and he was the one too stubborn to let go. But I was weak-minded and selfish for so long. And now I was paying for it. Taking a deep breath, I forced myself to look at him, my eyes heavy from the dense pressure of tears building up behind them.

"Pete." Biting my bottom lip, I held my eyes tight for a second before letting myself face my greatest mistake. "I just wanted to . . . apologize. For how I treated us." A few drops pooled at the corners of my eyes, streaking down my cheeks. "I did love you. I'm . . . still in love with you."

Pete's chest deflated as air escaped his nostrils. "I know." He swallowed, gaze shifting away momentarily. "I always knew you were."

"I know it's wrong because now Kala . . . " I shut my eyes to escape his. "You're with Kala. And it's too late and . . . I was stupid to think you'd wait. Stupid and . . . " The tears were coming strong now. I tried to control my breathing. Sorrow consumed me, making it hard to focus on anything but the negative thoughts my subconscious was feeding me.

Breathe in. Breathe out.

Pete's hands gently grasped my wrists, drawing me out of the torrent of my tears. Looking up, that superhero-level strength kept me from dropping to my knees. "I don't regret a thing. Not one second of it." He wiped my sadness away with careful fingers. "I forgive you, Ash. For all of it. Without you, I never would have got out of my funk with Mari. Never would have figured out my life. Never would have taken a chance. All of that was because of you." My lips trembled as he carried me with his gaze. "You're not the villain, Ash. You never were."

His arms wrapped around me, holding me against his chest as I let go of everything. He stroked the kinks of my loose hair, keeping me secured against him to let all the disappointments soak into the cotton of his shirt. "You're the Claire to my Andy." He leaned his cheek against my head.

A light chuckle leaked through, making me hold on to him tighter than ever. This moment would pass, like all the rest. This was just the start of me not screwing things up. It was raw, and it was scary as fuck, but it was how it should have always been. From the moment he kissed me at graduation, it should have always been this way. If only I had realized that before. But I didn't. And I would have to accept that and move on.

Drawing away but still keeping my hands at his sides, I looked up at his warm smile. "I'm glad you don't hate me."

"Nah, I could never hate you. Not for long, anyway." He sighed, rubbing my back slowly. "You gonna be okay?"

"I have to be."

"We're still friends? I don't want that to change."

"Yeah. Friends." I leaned away from him slowly, not wanting to relinquish what I knew I had already lost.

Pete's arms fell from my back. "Don't be too hard on Kala. You know she's gonna be super emotional when she finds out, you know."

"I won't." A deep breath lifted away the last few tears from my eyes. "You really like her, don't you?"

Pete's smile swelled to an unexpected level of bliss. "I do."

"I'll be on you if you treat her like shit."

"Trust me, I know." The corners of his mouth deflated into a settled grin. Reaching out his hand, he took mine, squeezing it into his palm. "I'll see ya, Ashley."

I squeezed back, a genuine smile crawling across my face. "Goodbye, Pete."

With a single motion, he leaned in, brushing his face against mine to leave a lasting kiss on my cheek. My eyes closed in silent serenity as he departed, relinquishing his hand from mine.

This chapter of my life was over. Unequivocally over. In the toughest way possible.

thirty-three

. . .

california, saturday, january 14th

IT TOOK a few days of crying before I left the apartment. I didn't think I'd ever cried so hard in my life. Not even for my dad. Work had to wait. The mere thought of facing Kala made my palms sweat. I didn't hate her and wasn't mad. I just didn't understand why she was afraid to tell me. It wasn't out of malice or a desire to showboat her victory over my failure. Because she didn't want to lose me as a friend? Of course, that was it. Despite that, a friend wouldn't keep that a secret.

When I finally got out of the apartment, the air was new. The sun's warmth on my cheeks was unlike anything I had felt before. I didn't have to go to work until tomorrow, but I had to for a different reason.

I sat on the ground outside, leaning against the windows of Starbucks. Korine's "Uncrossed" kept my blood pumping these last few days. I couldn't bear to listen to anything else, especially Joy Division. That would take forever for me to listen to again. I pulled at my black halter top, tossing my bag over my high-waisted jean shorts. It was almost time to open, and Kala always worked the morning shift on Saturdays.

I didn't have to wait too long before I heard her sneakers squeak on the sidewalk. She slid down the window to sit next to me, hair tied back, her plain work shirt on and apron hanging from her arms.

It was hard to look at her, but I caught her eye in my sullen state. "You could have told me."

She took a deep breath and blew it out slowly, her lips forming a perfect circle. "I know. I should have told you." Her eyes trembled as her words became regretful. "I'm a terrible friend."

Her impulse grasped my hand. She squeezed my palm so tightly I thought mine would break under the pressure. "You're my best friend, Ash. It scared me that you might never want to speak to me again."

"Kala, stop." I felt a tickle in the back of my throat. The desire to act over think would forever linger in my mind, but as much as this sucked, I couldn't *just* think about me. "I know I'll be happy for you. But this is a lot to process and . . . I need time to get over it."

The sadness stopped leaking from her eyes. "You're not mad?"

"Hurt. Not mad. And . . . a little upset you didn't tell me." I shook her hands and settled them between us. "Pete is fucking awesome. You two . . . are perfect for each other."

She sniffed, searching my face for any deception. "You don't mean that."

"Listen," I clenched my teeth and swallowed my self pity, "I love Pete. But . . . I can't just . . . love someone and hope they'll love me back. Especially after everything." I was in awe of my words, however riddled with regret they were. "You don't need to worry about me, okay? Worry about you and him."

"I just . . . I want you to be happy."

I could feel the last few puddles of my sadness reach the back of my eyes. Holding my breath, I let it straighten my posture in subtle triumph. "I have never been so in control of my life. That's enough for me right now."

Kala grasped on to me and I took her in, squeezing her so tight my eyes leaked their last drops. I couldn't find happiness at other people's expense. Using and abusing them like a paper doll in the wind. She deserved to be happy just as much as I did.

I might trip up, probably more than I would like. But the old Ashley was gone now. I didn't even recognize her anymore. And that was for the better. Because she was mean and out of control. This Ashley, the one holding on to someone who called me their hero, that Ashley was who I wanted to be.

"I love you, Ash," Kala murmured through her tears.

"I love you too." I drew away, taking a deep breath. "You have work, don't you?"

"Yeah." She sniffed, pressing her lips together as she wiped the wetness from her face. "You gonna be okay?"

"Come on, it's me. I'll be okay." I forced a smile.

"Okay." She moved her knees under her to stand. "Is it okay if I text you later?"

"Yeah. Sure."

Kala straightened her apron and walked around me. She took the handle, looking over at me one last time. With a weak smile, she swung open the door and stepped inside. I waited for it to drift back to its frame before curling my knees against my chest, leaning my forehead against them. Dragging my headphones back over my ears, I tapped them on, letting Jasper Byrne's "Bliss" scrape the bottom of the tears barrel.

Shit, that was hard. Facing Pete, how vulnerable I was. And Kala. The next step would be the most difficult one. Forgiving myself. It seemed impossible and also necessary. Almost as important as breathing.

But I had to forgive myself. For being confused. For handling it the way I did. Because I hadn't known any better and I had refused to take responsibility for my actions. It was as clear as the Midwest highways we took to get here. Instead of looking ahead, I looked in every other direction, mostly down, trying to retrace my steps.

They say time heals all wounds, but that wasn't true. Time gave me the opportunity to heal, and I had a choice to stay broken or put the pieces back together the best way I knew how. Or find new ones to replace those I'd lost.

I was getting there. Picking them up piece by piece.

A shadow moved in front of me, blocking the early morning glow of the sun. "Hey. Are you okay?"

My head shot up from my knees. A tall guy stood in front of me. His dark, deep-set eyes matched his hair, and he wore a pair of coal-washed jeans and a plain white tee. He had a red backpack hooked behind his shoulders. Something about him seemed familiar, but I couldn't quite think of who he might be.

"Yeah." I wiped my face with the back of my hand. "I mean . . . you know. Learning from my mistakes. Mending a broken heart."

"Wow. Most people just say 'yeah, sure' or 'I'm fine'." He bent down, balancing on the balls of his feet. "You're a fresh taste of reality."

I shrugged. "I'm trying something new."

He nodded assuredly. "Something everyone needs to try, if you ask me."

Now that he was closer, I remembered him. Pulling my headphones from my ears, I sniffed lightly as I loosened the hold around my knees. "You're Kaneda, right?"

"Yeah." He cracked a smile, like he was relieved I remembered him. "And just to be sure, you're Ashley?"

"Yeah." My genuine curiosity peaked. "So, what brings you?"

"Well, if you must know," he leaned his arms across his knees, "I was hoping you'd be working."

I shook my head, unable to rid the slight smirk his intentions brought to my face. "Nope. Sorry. Off duty today."

"Why are you sitting outside your work, then?" He shook his head, bringing his gaze away from my face. "Sorry. None of my business. You don't have to tell me."

"No, it's okay." I adjusted my posture to sit a little straighter. "I had to talk to someone."

"Oh, okay." A flash of uncertainty came over his otherwise calm expression as his eyes found mine again. "Well, if you're not busy, I was heading to the park to do some sketching. If you don't want to be alone, I mean."

"Oh." I squinted and shook my head. "I don't know."

"It's okay. No hard feelings." He rocked on his heels to stand. "I'll leave you be."

I watched him adjust his shirt before taking a step back. "Wait." He stopped and looked down at me. "Why do you want me to come with you?"

He shrugged, letting go of some nervous energy. "If we're talking about being honest here, I've been trying to think of a way to ask you out for a while now."

I let the seconds tick by, twisting my mouth as I mulled over this opportunity. This guy barely knew me, only that I made an excellent macchiato. But maybe that was a good thing. "You don't have to be nice to me."

"Well, I don't want to be a jerk."

"Humph." A smirk formed. "I'm from New York. I'm used to jerks."

"Didn't you know?" His smile took over. "Us Cali guys are a whole different breed."

"Is that so?" I clenched my mouth as I peered down at my knees. I still wasn't sure if I deserved this. He wasn't cheeky like Pete or slick like Wes, but a little of both. He had a coolness about him I could only compare to Bruce Lee in *Fist of Fury*, that exuded finesse without needing to try very hard. And I was always a sucker for a guy with a killer smile. Before I could contemplate further, Kaneda's hand appeared in front of me.

"Can I at least help you up?"

I lost all control of my facial muscles. Without thinking too much about it, I took his hand, and I slowly ascended. He didn't linger in my palm and pulled away like a gentleman should when talking to a girl for the first time. Well, not for the first time. But a conversation other than coffee.

I adjusted my bag, leaning to my left. "You're not a stalker, are you?"

"Stalker? Me? Oh no, no. You've got the wrong guy." He hooked his thumb in his jean loop.

"Your attitude might change about me the more you get to know me."

"I'm willing to take a chance." His hands came up, palms forward. "I don't want to make you uncomfortable. Just two people. Hanging out. I won't draw you or anything creepy like that."

"What if I wanted you to draw me?" I asked, tilting my head above my shoulder.

He shrugged. "I'm cool with that."

I studied him carefully, my heart taking a few extra beats as his subtle charm ate away at me. Kaneda's eyes brightened, another smile patiently waiting for my dismissal or acceptance of his proposal.

Goosebumps prickled up my arms as my heart kept time in my ears. I moved my head back to my center. Pete was out of reach now, and that was that. I had been too late, and he was already hand in hand with someone else. Someone deserving of him and vice versa. I would never forget what he had done for me. What he gave me, I would carry with me forever. But to be stuck in what could have been, that was what got me into this mess. I had to break the pattern.

Taking a step forward, I moved around him as he followed me with his eyes. "Don't say I didn't warn you."

Kaneda turned, the charm leaking into his already alluring smile. One I could totally get used to. "You're really that bad?"

"Guess you'll have to find out."

We walked toward the park together, side by side.

Nothing may come of this. And it was okay to be afraid. But if I didn't move forward, I'd be standing in one place forever. And that was way scarier than taking the first step.

the following year

pete, wyoming, tuesday, july 20th

Devils Tower looks bigger than the last time we were here. It's July and the summers are brutal once the sun is highest in the sky, so choosing to walk the trail early was ideal.

Ashley sits on a large boulder overlooking the plains. Khaki shorts and a loose fitted tie dye tee showing off her midriff, which donned a denim fanny pack. Her signature pink aviator sunglasses sat over her smooth beige face. She adjusted the two buns on either side of her ears, resembling Princess Lea.

It's weird trying to compare her to the girl she was a year ago. The last time we were here wasn't exactly fun. She told me she wanted to try. Told me she was done pushing me away. We kissed as the sun rose alongside Devils Tower, and I could tell she was telling the truth for once. I felt it. But then, it all went to shit. And in the heat of the moment, I screwed up just like she did. And everything we shared came crashing down as quickly as we built it up.

It took a lot of time to realize that we wouldn't make it then. She was too broken, and I couldn't keep my promise to handle the aftershock. It hurt knowing I couldn't help her. Because I wanted to.

Even though she said I did, I knew I couldn't be everything she needed. Or she wouldn't have lied about Axel. And I wouldn't have given up.

So, now we're here, sitting side by side on a boulder, overlooking this incredible representation of no-man's-land, Wyoming. It isn't easy coming back. But, a lot changed since then. And this girl, sitting next to me, isn't that same broken girl anymore.

She looks at me. As soon as her head tilts to the right over her shoulder, I can't stop myself from smiling. I still love when she looks at me like that. I don't think that will ever change for as long as we stay friends.

"What are you thinking about, Andy?"

She still calls me Andy a lot. Ever since we adopted the Breakfast Club personae's in high school. I am Andy and she's Claire. At least most of the time.

I shrug, trying to keep the memories from getting the better of me. "Just last time we were here."

"Oh," she looks down at the dread cut of her tie dye shirt, "yeah, I guess it's hard not to think about that."

She brings her suntanned legs onto the rock, crossing them against the hard surface. "I can't believe we're still friends sometimes."

"Hey," I say abruptly, trying to stop her from falling down the rabbit hole of regret. "We're okay now."

Her hands drop to her sides as she looks back at me.

Could I have done things differently? Of course, I could have. She could have, too. I left her in her brother's apartment, hoping to spare myself the pain of knowing how much she cried. It was hard to leave things the way we did and distance myself from her to get my heart back to how it was. Before I fell in love with her.

I can't pinpoint when I knew I loved her. Maybe when we talked under the bleachers during Chris' track meet. Or when she showed me her stash of secret kittens in the mall alleyway. It might have been that very night I stepped in between her and Westley. I felt a surge of emotions as I saw Ashley in the hallway that day, unlike any I had ever felt before.

"Pete." Ashley's lips fold in between her teeth. "Seriously. Why didn't you write me off?"

The question makes me more nervous than I realize. I hold nothing against Ash for what happened. We both had a part to play, and we each played it poorly. I knew what I was getting myself into with her from the beginning, but being prepared for it was another thing all together. I can't condemn her for her shortcomings. Do I wish she tried harder? Hell yes, I do. But she didn't and here we are. Two former lovers recovered from the choppy seas of a relationship gone wrong. Each of us is better for it. Especially Ash. If I didn't know who she was before, I would never have thought she could be anything but the understanding, supportive friend she is now.

I glance down at my basketball shorts and fitted Batman tee, stopping my glasses from sliding down the sweaty surface of my nose. "I've answered this question already."

"No. You've avoided answering it." She slides closer to me. "How much longer do you think you can keep me waiting?"

A sigh escapes me. I push a few loose strands of my dirty blond hair under my bandana. "I guess . . . I have a hard time letting go of things."

Her brow arches. "You guess?"

"Alright." I smirk. "I have a hard time. Did. Have a harder time . . . back then. And maybe I should have just dropped you." My mouth twists as I contemplate my next words. "People say it's hard to forget your first love. And I guess they're right. Because I can't forget you. Even though I don't love you the same, I still want you in my life." I bring my shoulders up as I shake my head. "Is that selfish? Probably."

The sounds of the wilderness filter in with the silence that follows my definitive answer. Ash watches me, her eyes carefully scanning over my features like she's trying to catch me in a lie.

I wait with anticipation for her to say something, but the more she looks me over, the more my mouth stretches into a smile. I assumed she was mimicking me because her smile was identical to mine. The next thing I know, we break into a sudden fit of laughter. Her hand comes off the rock and rests on my arm as I pull with my head back to project into the sky.

A few minutes pass before we settle. But her hand doesn't leave me. "You were so nervous. It was adorable."

I exhale through my nose, releasing the last remains of uncertainty from my chest. "Yeah, well. The truth isn't always easy."

She squeezes my arm. "I'm glad you're selfish. I'm glad we're okay. And . . . " her hand slides down onto the warm stone, "I'm glad you found someone who could be everything I couldn't be for you."

Damn it. The old Ashley would have chewed my words and spit them back in some harsh, accusatory way. I had to stop thinking she would ever go back to that. Trust was the last thing left to rebuild between us. We had smashed a lot of that to smithereens, Incredible Hulk style. I knew it wasn't impossible for someone to come back a better person. But seeing is believing in some circumstances. And this is seeing, front and center, how much better a person she'd become.

"I care about you a lot, Pete."

"I know." I reach my arm out around her, coaxing her into a hug. Her chin rests on my shoulder as we pull our bodies together. I don't think it will ever feel wrong to hold her. I couldn't ask for a better person to remain in my life. Even if this is all we were. Haters to lovers to friends. What a weird track to ride on. But we did it. And looking back, despite everything, it wasn't such a terrible trip.

"You're the Claire to my Andy," I tell her as I breathe in the Mediterranean scent of her hair. "No one can replace you."

"Good." We pull away from each other. "'Cause I'm not going anywhere."

"Hey."

Both our heads turn. My eyes fall on the copper-skinned beauty that is my Kala. Her hair is in a ponytail, swishing against the bare top of her shoulders. She had on a simple tank top and olive hiking shorts. A retro neon pull-string pack strapped under her arms.

"Sorry, I know you guys needed a minute, but Kaneda just ate it on the rocks up there."

"Uh oh." I look over at Ash with a matter-of-fact expression. "We better go rescue your," I lift my hands and air quote my next word, "'date'."

Ash rolls her eyes and shoves me before hopping off the rock. "Shut up, Pete."

I grab my water bottle and follow suit. "You've been dating for how long now?"

"Ha ha ha. You're so funny." She eyes me with a sly turn of her head. "And none of your business."

"It's been at least . . . nine months," Kala added.

"Kala." Ash eyes her playfully, gently pinching her arm. "Aren't you supposed to be on my side?"

"How is pretending you two aren't an item helping you?" Kala smirks, following her as she passes. "I think inviting him on a road trip to Wyoming crosses the bridge to *official* by now!"

Ash waves her hand in the air and continues up the path. When Kala turns back to me, my heart practically switches to ludicrous speed. Her smile doesn't wash from her face, her soft eyes sparkling in the new day sun.

It's been over a year since I officially asked her out. We had a few awkward months before that, considering the circumstances of how we met. Every day still feels like the first date. I feel lighter. Like I'm supposed to be better. Always laughing. Always smiling. Each day is an adventure when we're together. A fun, no holds barred journey of epic proportions.

It took a lot of contemplating to realize how much I'd fallen for her after Ashley. Part of me felt guilty for dragging her into our shit. Kala was so innocent. And both Ash and I were so corrupt. But things happen for a reason, or so I have finally resigned myself to believe. Because if I never took a chance with Ash, I would have never met *the one*. And I am convinced that Kala is. My person.

"You guys okay?" she asks as I slip my arm around her waist and hold her to me.

"Yeah, we're always okay."

Kala nuzzles into my chest. The midsummer scent of her honey perfume mixed with sunscreen makes my heart race.

"I still feel guilty sometimes," Kala glances up at me, "about everything."

I run my hand up to her shoulder, moving a few stray strands of her dark hair behind her ear. "You might." My thumb comes to rest under her chin, tilting her beautiful face toward mine. "But that doesn't change how I feel. Things happen. Nobody's perfect. But I wouldn't change a thing. You know that, right?"

Waiting is hard when she's so close to me, and I don't give her a chance to speak before kissing her sun-drenched lips. Her hand comes up to take my face, giving us a few more seconds to bask before we part.

"I can't get enough of you. I don't want to be without this. Ever."

Her breathless smile fills me to bursting. "Same."

I slide in front of her, bending my knees before giving her the okay to hop on. She happily jumps onto my back, gluing her legs to my sides as I wrap my arms around them to support her. Her head rests on my shoulder and her hands loosely lock around my neck as I take her up the path to where Ash disappeared.

I don't have to walk too far before both Ash and Kaneda come into view. He leans against the side of the ridge in a loose-fitted green tank, drawstring shorts, and a large bandage across his left knee. A wave of dark hair falls against the side of his face. Ash's neck strains as she reaches up to meet his lips, his hands tenderly holding her face.

I was a little weary of Kaneda when I first met him. I didn't want him to turn out to be a complete douchebag like Wes. There is still this lingering instinct to protect Ash that I need to get over. But the caution didn't last long. I might not like everything about the guy, but I can tell how crazy he is about Ash. He treats her right. And she is happy. More than she will ever admit.

Kala leans into my ear. "They look so perfect together."

"Yeah," I breathe through a smile, "they do, don't they?"

I guess I can say I am head-over-heels for life right now. Yeah. It's pretty sweet. And it can only get better.

The End

acknowledgments

wow. wow. wow. wow.

There are no words for seeing this finally come to a close. Pete and Ashley were "the first" for a reason. I hope I told it well, through all the kisses and stones and secrets and spice. Their story was a ride down nostalgia road that sent my young teenage heart a-pounding each and every time. Remembering the pressures of high school, the petty fights with friends, the boys that broke my heart, and the ones that embraced it.

Firstly, I want to say thank you to my amazing editor, Nicolette Beebe, who, through her enthusiasm and genuine care, really helped make writing this book so much more satisfying. It's been a hell of a ride for Pete and Ashley, and I am so happy you were there right along with me.

To my amazing cover designer, Sara Oliver, and my proof/line editor, Chelsea. They say a successful book is created by the team behind it. And I honestly think I found the perfect one to support me in writing this duology.

To the amazing artist, Ana Velia, who has brought the characters of this duology alive again and again. It has been so incredible collaborating with you these last two years. Thank you so much for all the time and effort you put into your work, all while attending school. You are a rock star!

To all those who supported me through social media. You know who you are. Kacey, Joanna, Rebecca, Lilian, Mary, Katie, Amanda, Jo, Jennifer, Jodi, JD (a lot of J's) and the rest of the community I've had to pleasure of meeting are worth all the algorithm changes and mistaken strikes. I love seeing your successes unfold and am so happy to have connected with all of you in our journeys to authordom.

To the musical artists that practically wrote this book for me. So much inspiration and emotion came from listening to your wonderful work while I sat at my desk or phone, banging out these hopeful, broken-hearted chapters. You helped mold my characters, create the conflict, bitter moments, and passionate kisses that exist in these pages. I will list all the artists that I listened to on repeat at the end of this rant.

And last, but certainly not least, to my one and only. Despite my resistance to letting you step into my world of writing, you never once told me I was wasting my time. I might not write the genres you like, but you've always been in my corner. Thank you for keeping things real and making me laugh along the way.

And to you, dear reader. Books would not need to be written without people to read them. I am grateful you gave this book a chance to make you feel something, whatever that something may be.

Okay, rant concluded.

Check out these incredible musical artists who took me on a ride to creative success. Seriously, I *could not* write without them. They inspired me to weave words and create meaning behind them:

The Midnight

M83

Timecop1983

Six Leaves Left

Immortal Girlfriend

Korine

Radiohead

Jasper Byrne

Chvrches

The 1975

Joy Division

Kate Bush

secrets & spice playlist

Here are the artists/albums that were mentioned throughout the novel. Be sure to check out each and every one of these amazing artists, past and present. And you can listen to the official Secrets & Spice playlist on my YouTube channel or on Spotify.

M83 - HurryUp, We'reDreaming
Pink Floyd - The Wall
The Backstreet Boys - Backstreet's Back
The Crystals - Then He Kissed Me
The 1975 - I like it When You Sleep, For You are So Beautiful Yet so Unaware of it
Chvrches - The Bones of What You Believe
Immortal Girlfriend - Daybreak EP
Radiohead - Pablo Honey
Whitney Houston - Whitney
Joy Division - Unknown Pleasures
Kate Bush - Running Up That Hill
Six Leave Left - We Were Brave
Iron & Wine - The Shepherd's Dog

Jasper Byrne - Night
Korine - Uncrossed

226

about the author

D. Allyson Howlett is a millennial wordsmith from urban Long Island, New York and currently residing in a small farm town in New Hampshire. She is passionate about nachos, creating music playlists, and watching Wednesday night pro-wrestling with her family.

Secrets & Spice is the final book in *A Playlist Kinda Love Story* series. This is her third published work and second novel.

also by d. allyson howlett

Kisses & Stones: A Playlist Kinda Love Story, Side A

Spirits n' Chai

Thank you so much for reading! If you are feeling generous, please leave a review on Goodreads or wherever you purchased this book. Reviews are an indie authors bread and butter and I would greatly appreciate it!

D. Allyson Howlett

www.dallysonhowlett.com

www.linktr.ee/d.allyson_writes

9 798985 281040